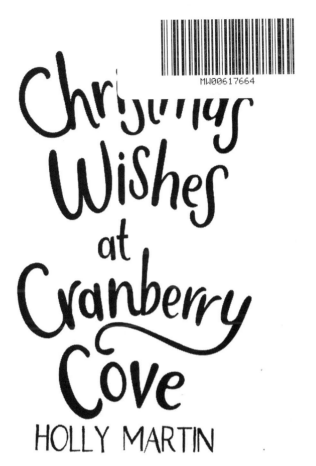

Christmas Wishes at Cranberry Cove

HOLLY MARTIN

CHAPTER ONE

December 20th

Orla Kennedy looked around the room with a smile. Carrie and Antonio had rented a beautiful, converted barn in the next town of White Cliff Bay for their wedding. It had been a small, casual affair for family and close friends and she liked that she'd been part of that. The room had been decorated perfectly with Christmas trees, garlands of holly, pinecones and berries. There were table arrangements of white candles surrounded by ivy and berries too, plus an abundance of white twinkling fairy lights everywhere. There'd even been a festive-themed buffet with mince pies and Christmas pudding flavoured scones. It was just a week until Christmas, so it was the perfect event to get everyone in the festive mood.

Carrie looked so happy and in love and Orla couldn't

have been more delighted that she'd found love after all those years alone.

Orla was sitting at a table with her closest friends; Carrie's daughter Fern, her husband Fletcher and their daughter Ocean, a very heavily pregnant Roo, who was married to Carrie's son Theo, and Ettie who was with her husband, Tom. Their two children had gone to their grandparents for the weekend, so Ettie was more than a little tipsy as she enjoyed her weekend of freedom.

And then there was Shay, Carrie's other son. Her childhood best friend and the love of her life. She was an idiot, she had been in love with this man since she'd met him when she was fourteen and he was never going to be hers, he just didn't see her in that way. Although he didn't know that part, she'd kept that hidden for years. There was a time she thought he'd felt the same, but not anymore. No matter how hard she tried, she couldn't let go of her love for him. She'd dated other people and so had he but she could never really move on from him. But having him in her life as a friend, her best friend, was infinitely better than not having him in her life at all. She'd been there and she definitely didn't want to go back to that again.

He looked magnificent tonight, dressed In a suit with a red tie. He was such a big man, in height and breadth, everything about him was strong and muscular. He had gentle grey eyes and a beautiful smile that not many people got to see.

Everyone started getting up to dance and as her table almost completely emptied, she knew Shay would ask her to dance. Whenever they went to an event, a charity ball or some other kind of party she always ended up dancing with Shay. If she was sensible, she'd say no when he asked, save herself the heartache of being held in his arms knowing he'd never be hers, but she couldn't do it. Those few minutes were pure bliss and she relished every second being held against him. So she put up with the pain of unrequited love and tortured herself with moments like dancing with him because being held in his arms was heaven even if it was only ever platonic.

Ettie squeezed her hand as she walked past. 'Sorry to abandon you, but I think someone lovely will probably ask you to dance soon.'

Ettie winked and smiled as she moved onto the dance floor with Tom.

Orla should probably have been embarrassed that everyone noticed that she always danced with Shay, but she was used to people talking about them by now. All their friends and family were always making comments about the two of them. They spent so much time together, at work and outside of it, that everyone was always trying to matchmake the two of them together. But Shay would always dismiss it, tell people they were just friends, and so she did the same.

As predicted, he stood up and moved over to her, offering out a hand. 'Would you like to dance?'

'Of course.'

She took his hand, and he led her onto the dance floor, not caring that everyone seemed to be watching the two of them. She placed one hand on his shoulder and one hand in his. She let out a tiny gasp of delight when he moved his other hand round her back and his fingers grazed her bare skin. Maybe she was guilty of choosing a dress that was almost backless for that reason. He stroked his fingers up and down her spine and her heart thundered in her chest at his gentle touch. She looked up at him and for a moment she thought she'd seen his eyes darken with desire before she dismissed it. She was seeing what she wanted to see.

She closed her eyes and rested her head on his chest, relishing in the feel of his arms wrapped around her, pretending for a moment that all of this was real.

'You look beautiful tonight, Orla,' Shay said, softly as they moved around the dance floor.

She looked up at him. 'Thank you, and you always look amazing in a suit. If I had my way, being manager of the Little Beach Hut Hotel would require you to wear a suit every day.'

'Thankfully, you're not in charge of the dress code and being manager means I can choose what I want to wear and be a bit more casual if I want, but if wearing a suit makes you happy, maybe I should wear one more often.'

She smiled up at him. God she so wanted to lean up and kiss him right now and it had nothing to do with the glass of mulled wine she'd had a while before. 'You make me happy regardless of what you wear.'

He stared at her and she wondered if she had pushed it too far.

'I just meant I'm grateful to have you in my life. We've been friends for so long and then we weren't and now we are again and I'm grateful that you were able to look past the silly immature teenager I was and let me back into your life again.'

'I loved the girl you were when we met, just as I love the woman you are now.'

Her heart leapt so hard it felt like it had catapulted into her throat. She studied him for a moment, trying to get a read from his face. 'You mean you love me as a friend?'

He shrugged. 'You take it any way you want to take it.'

She frowned in confusion. 'What does that mean?'

He sighed. 'Maybe it's being at a wedding, watching two people who are so happy together, who love each other completely commit to spending the rest of their lives together and it makes me feel sad that I've never found that. Or if I'm being truthful, I was never brave enough to go after it. Orla, I—'

Just then Roo and Theo danced into their space. 'May we cut in,' Roo said.

Orla looked at Roo in surprise and, if she was honest, a little bit of frustration. She loved her friend dearly but now was not the time for whatever this was.

But Shay, looking equally frustrated, nodded politely and after a few awkward moments, they swapped dancing partners so she was dancing with Theo.

'Sorry for the interruption,' Theo said.

'It's OK,' Orla said, even though it really wasn't, but then maybe it was a good thing. What Shay had been saying was starting to give her hope and that was a dangerous road to go down.

'We just wanted to say that you and Shay are important to us and with our son due in the next few weeks, we wanted to ask if you would be his godparent. With Shay, Fern and Fletcher of course.

Her frustration was immediately forgotten. 'Oh, wow, of course. I'd be honoured. Thank you.'

'No, thank you. There's so much to think about when bringing a child into the world and we just wanted to get this sorted now, just in case anything should happen to us.'

'I'm touched to be asked. Are you getting excited?'

'Probably nervous more than anything, we just want to do the best for him.'

'You will. He has two parents who love each other completely and utterly and will love him with that same ferocity. He can't ask for more than that.'

He nodded. 'Since Roo came back into my life, everything just makes so much sense. Having a child with her makes sense, I want to build a future with her. There's a tiny part of me that worries that because I had such a terrible upbringing, what kind of father would I be to my son, but I love him so much already and he hasn't even been born yet. I know I will do everything in my power to make sure he is loved and cared for.'

'Your son is going to be the luckiest boy in the world having you two as parents. And you have nothing to worry about. You're one of the kindest, most generous and selfless people I know. You gave up being CEO of a multi-million-pound company to be CEO of a wildlife animal rescue instead. If you can do that for animals, imagine how much love your son will get.'

Theo smiled. 'Thank you.'

She smiled and glanced over at Shay as he chatted with Roo. Everything about being with Shay made sense too. They just clicked in a way that she didn't have with anyone else, not even Fern, Roo or Ettie. She saw him every day, as she managed and ran Seahorses, the café that was part of The Little Beach Hut Hotel. As the manager at the hotel, he was always popping in and would often come for breakfast or lunch, but she knew it was more than just convenience of using the café where he worked, she knew he enjoyed spending time with her too.

A lot of people assumed they were already a couple as they were so close, and those that knew they weren't would often ask why, as it was apparently obvious to anyone looking in that they were both in love with each other. But she knew the truth. Shay didn't love her like that. Maybe he loved her as a friend but not the passionate, head over heels in love feelings she felt for him. He'd told her that himself.

Unless things had changed.

'You know, when Roo first came back to Apple Hill Bay, I phoned Shay and asked him what I should do,' Theo said, dragging her attention back to him. 'He said I had to tell Roo how I felt for her when we were teenagers. I'd never told her I loved her before she left which was my biggest regret. I didn't see the point as it had been fourteen years since I'd last seen her, it was water under the bridge. Why make things awkward and weird between us for something that was in the past. But Shay said that we had to start with a clean slate and the only way forward was if she knew the truth. I'm so glad I listened to him, because it turned out she'd felt the same way. Sometimes you have to be brave, take a risk.'

'And sometimes doing that can ruin everything.'

Theo sighed. 'Shay's past is a complicated one. And the man's an idiot. Well, he used to be in the past, fortunately he's grown out of all that, well… most of it.'

Orla's cheeks flushed with embarrassment. 'He told you, what happened that weekend?'

Theo paused before he answered, clearly realising he'd said something he shouldn't. 'Yes but only very recently, a few weeks ago in fact. But I haven't told anyone, not even Roo. And you have nothing to be embarrassed about. What you did was brave and courageous and I'm sorry it ended the way that it did.'

She shook her head. 'It's in the past. I don't want to talk about it.'

'Maybe you should. With Shay not me.'

'I'm a big fan of not rocking the boat.'

Theo sighed and the song came to an end.

'Thanks for the dance,' Orla said, stepping out of his arms.

'I'm sorry, it wasn't my place to say anything.'

She nodded, still a bit miffed that Shay had told Theo about it after all this time. Why bring it up now?

'It's getting hot in here, I need to get a drink.' She nodded her thanks to Theo and walked over to the bar.

She ordered a glass of wine and took a sip as she surveyed the room. What could she possibly gain about talking about that weekend with Shay again? She wanted to forget it had ever happened. It was twelve years ago after all.

Roo came over. 'Theo said he thinks he might have upset you. Are you OK?'

She'd never told Roo or anyone what had happened that weekend, she'd been too humiliated for that, so she could hardly bring it up now. 'I'm fine.' She decided to change the subject. 'Thank you for asking me to be godparent to your son, I'm honoured you would think of me.'

'Of course, I love you, we all do. And we just want you to be happy,' Roo said, meaningfully.

'I am happy. I live in one of the most beautiful parts of the world, I love my job running Seahorses, I have wonderful friends. I don't need more than that.'

She ignored the ache in her heart that said otherwise.

'That was a lovely party,' Orla said, looking through the car window as Shay drove them home. It was snowing hard, settling on the clifftop road, and the grassy verges. It was likely they'd have a few inches of the stuff by tomorrow morning, which would make getting to work interesting. She was holding out hope that it would last another week so they could have a white Christmas for the first time in a long time. They so rarely got snow on the coast, so this was very exciting.

She looked over at Shay as he drove back along the coastal road towards her house. She had danced with Shay again later at the wedding reception, but he hadn't said anything more and she hadn't questioned him about what he'd been trying to say earlier. She didn't want to bring it up to then find out she'd completely misunderstood. She'd rather just not know.

He looked at her and smiled. 'It was. I had a great night. Did you want to come back to mine for a coffee?' He gestured to the turn off for his house, which sat on the cliff tops overlooking Cranberry Cove. 'Ivy will be delighted to see you.'

Ivy was his five-month-old newfoundland puppy that was already the size of a small horse. She knew Shay had already popped home three times to check on her during the course of the wedding and reception. Ivy was deaf and the reason why her owners had dumped her. She had been tied to the gates of Little Paws, Theo's wildlife rescue centre with a note that said, 'She's deaf, the vet wanted to charge me four hundred pounds to put her down so you can deal with it.' The note hadn't even bothered to say her name obviously thinking she wasn't worth saving. An hour later she had found a new forever home with Shay. She had the sweetest nature and Orla loved playing with her, but even Shay's beautiful dog would not be enough to make her go to his house.

'Oh no, thanks, I better get back, I have to be up early for the café.'

He nodded and she glanced out the window so she wouldn't have to look at him. She sighed as she felt the awkwardness of her refusal. Although she could torture herself by dancing with him, there was a line she wouldn't cross and that was going to his house. She never wanted to go back to Starlight Cottage. There were too many memories there that hurt too much. Shay had bought the cottage off Antonio around eighteen months before, after Antonio had moved in with Carrie and finally decided to sell it. Orla had successfully refused every invite to go there ever since but there would come a point when Shay would ask why.

'Can I ask why you keep refusing to come to my house?'

She pulled a face. Clearly that point had arrived.

'I don't. You know I'm always busy with the café,' she lied.

'You've not been there once. Is it because of... what happened there?'

She let out a little gasp; they'd agreed never to speak about it. Despite trying to push those memories away, she could remember that weekend so vividly, every little detail. Why was he bringing it up again? Why did he talk about it with Theo?

'No, it's just—'

She saw a movement out of her window, and she looked out the windscreen at the shadow that was fast approaching.

'Deer!' she yelled as the stag leapt across the road.

Shay swerved, skidded on the snow on the side of the road and the car tumbled over the edge of the cliff.

She screamed as the car plummeted down the steep grassy bank. Shay desperately tried to regain control of the car but there was too much snow and the car spun around as it bounced off rocks. She could see the white froth of the high tide crashing on the sands as they plunged towards the beach way too fast.

They hit the beach headfirst with a deafening bang, the air bags exploded, the windscreen smashed and water poured into the car. A large wave crashed against the car, tossing the car on its side. Orla smacked her head hard and everything went black.

CHAPTER TWO

Orla, aged 14. December 8th

Orla stood at the top of the cliffs looking down at the three beaches that made up Apple Hill Bay: Strawberry Sands directly under her, Blackberry Beach in the middle of the bay and opposite, the beautiful secluded Cranberry Cove.

Cranberry Cove was one of her favourite places to go, especially after dark, because no one else went there. At low tide, the public steps to the beach were dark and treacherous and at high tide, the only access to the cove was from the steps at the back of Starlight Cottage, the little holiday let that sat alone on the clifftops over the little beach. Someone had put solar lights along the private steps which made it easier to traverse in the dark.

The cottage, despite its prime location, was very rarely rented out, probably due to its exorbitant price, so sneaking into the garden to access the steps had never been a problem. When it was occupied, it was a little harder, but not impossible. But someone had stayed there for the last few weeks and spent most evenings in the garden, which had put a stop to her illicit trespassing. There had been no sign of a car there over the last few days so she might be able to go back to her favourite spot again tonight.

She liked it there because it was so quiet. No shouting, no screaming, no vases or mugs being thrown or smashed across the room, it was just the gentle sound of the waves lapping on the sand; it was the peace she so desperately craved.

Her parents hated each other. Not enough that they wanted to leave, but enough that they wanted to make each other's lives a living hell. Of course that meant her life was a living hell too. She was dreading Christmas this year and Christmas was normally her favourite time of year.

When her family had lived in Ireland, her dad had ruined a seemingly perfect happy marriage by having an affair. After swearing it was a mistake and it would never happen again, they'd all moved to England to start a new life, but her mum could never trust him again and after a few months her dad had another affair with the mum of Roo, one of the girls from school. They'd been shouting and screaming ever since and she stayed out of the house as often as she could despite the cold December weather.

'Hey!'

Orla turned to see who was calling her and smiled to see Fern, the new girl at school. She had only been at their school for a few weeks but there was something so likeable and endearing about her.

'Hi Fern.'

'Hey, do you live round here?'

'Not far from here, just a few minutes' walk down towards the main part of the town. My house overlooks the harbour, but I just like the view from up here.'

'It's beautiful, isn't it? I live over there,' Fern pointed to the stone cottage. 'So I wake up to that view every day. Do you want to come back to mine for a bit? Mum makes the best mince pies.'

Oh, to have a mum that cared enough to make mince pies. Orla's own mum barely even knew she was there; she was too busy arguing with her dad to notice Orla's comings or goings let alone have time to make mince pies. But Fern was looking at her so hopefully she didn't have the heart to say she was too bitter and twisted to play happy families with someone else's mum.

'Sure, that would be nice,' Orla said, and Fern's face split into a huge smile as she gestured for Orla to follow her. 'So, you're enjoying living here?'

'I love it,' said Fern. 'I go to the beach every day, what's not to love about that? First time I even saw the beach was when I moved here, now I never want to leave.'

Orla smiled at that. 'Any brothers or sisters move with you?'

'Two brothers, Theo and Shay. They are always off surfing, so I think they love it here too.'

'So just the five of you?'

Orla was diplomatically trying to find out if Fern's parents were still together without asking if they were bitterly at each other's throats like her own parents were. She imagined if Fern's mum was happily making mince pies, then her dad would be the sort that would be making treehouses in the garden.

'Four.'

'Your parents aren't together?' It would be nice to find a kindred spirit in that regard.

'Oh, I have no idea who my dad is,' Fern said. 'He was never part of my life. My birth mum didn't want to be part of my life either, I haven't seen her since I was seven, which is how I ended up in foster care, but Carrie adopted me about a year ago.'

Orla felt guilt and shame flood through her. It was so easy to assume everyone else had a perfect rose-tinted life, but everyone had their own issues and their own emotional baggage to deal with.

'I'm sorry.'

'Don't be, I have the best mum in the world with Carrie,' Fern said, cheerfully. 'Come on, you can meet her for yourself.'

Fern let herself into her kitchen and Orla followed. There was a woman standing at the oven, presumably making their dinner. She turned when she heard the door opening and a big smile lit up her face.

'Hello, my darling,' Carrie said, opening her arms and Fern stepped straight into them without any of the embarrassment that most of Orla's teenage friends would have. Orla swallowed a lump in her throat. She would love to have a hug from her own mum but love and affection had been severely lacking from their relationship in recent years. 'Did you have a good day in school?'

'Yeah, I did,' Fern's voice was muffled as her face was pressed into Carrie's chest.

Fern stepped back and Carrie spotted Orla.

'Who's this?'

'This is my friend Orla,' Fern said.

To Orla's surprise, Carrie came over and gave her a big hug too and that made all kinds of emotions swirl in her chest. It had been a long time since she'd been held like this. 'Lovely to meet you. You're staying for dinner, right?'

'Oh, I erm...' Orla said. But then what was waiting for her at home? She'd probably make herself a bacon sandwich or cheese on toast. There certainly wasn't going to be any lovingly prepared home-cooked meal. 'If that's OK.'

Fern nodded.

'Of course it is, as long as it's OK with your parents,' Carrie said.

'I'll text Mum,' Orla said, knowing full well she wouldn't get a reply.

'Well help yourselves to cakes or mince pies, I've just got to make a few phone calls,' Carrie said, gesturing to the cake tin before hurrying out.

'Your mum's pretty cool,' Orla said, looking around at the Christmas tree twinkling with lights in the corner. There were already presents stacked neatly underneath and festive garlands strewn around the room. Christmas songs were playing on the radio and the scent of mince pies and gingerbread cookies filled the air. Her parents hadn't even bothered decorating for Christmas this year and there certainly wouldn't be any home-made mince pies or Christmas cookies.

Fern nodded. 'Yes, she is.' She looked at something out the window and rolled her eyes. 'Oh, here come my brothers. Theo will probably flirt with you, he's like that with everyone, so don't take it personally. Shay probably won't say anything to you, he's like that with everyone too.'

Orla turned round to see two strong, good-looking boys laughing and walking up to the door. They arrived in the kitchen with a lot of noise and chaos and damp clothes. She'd seen them both before around the town and on the beach, but she hadn't spoken to either of them. They both stopped when they saw Orla.

'Oh hello,' one of them said.

'Hello, I'm Orla.'

'Oh, I love your accent,' he said. 'I'm Theo and this is Shay.'

Shay stared at her but didn't say anything. Fern had summed them up perfectly. Orla recognised Shay from the ice cream shop. He'd started working there a few weeks ago. He was so at odds there with their colourful displays, counters filled with a multitude of bright flavoured ice creams and lots of sprinkles. It was everything he wasn't, with his permanent scowl and dark clothes.

'Theo, you're bleeding,' Fern gasped.

Orla looked at Theo's t-shirt and could see blood seeping through on his side.

'It's just a scratch,' Theo said.

'It's a bit more than that,' Shay said.

'I'm going to try and clean it up a bit before Mum sees it,' Theo said, walking out the kitchen, completely unfazed.

A few seconds later it was evident he had failed at that mission.

'Oh my god,' Carrie almost screamed.

Fern went running out to see the wound for herself, leaving Orla alone with Shay.

They stared at each other. He really was exceptionally good-looking.

'You live at Windmill Cottage, right?' Shay said.

She frowned. 'How do you know that?'

'I walk past there sometimes on my way back from my job in the ice cream shop. I hear your parents screaming at each other and sometimes I see you, sitting in the lounge or your bedroom trying to block it all out. I've often thought about marching in there, taking you by the hand and marching back out again.'

She stared at him in shock. No one had noticed what was going on in her house, or if they had they certainly hadn't cared enough to ask her about it. But this stranger, this boy who she'd never spoken to, he cared. He cared enough to want to get her out of there.

Shay looked embarrassed that he'd said that. 'But then I figured some stranger basically abducting you from your house would probably scare you, and your parents probably wouldn't be happy about it either.'

'My parents wouldn't even notice you were there, or that I wasn't. They're far too busy shouting at each other.'

'I'm sorry. I know what it's like being in the middle of a very toxic relationship.'

'Well next time you're passing, feel free to come and break me out,' Orla said.

His mouth twitched in a smile.

Carrie marched back into the kitchen, almost dragging a reluctant Theo with her.

'I need to take Theo to get some stitches,' Carrie said.

'Mum, it's fine, just a scratch,' Theo protested.

'Shay, can you give the girls some dinner? The meatballs are nearly ready, the pasta needs putting on now and there's garlic bread in the fridge that needs heating up. Monica will be collecting Fern in half an hour for her painting class so can you walk Orla home?' Carrie said, completely ignoring Theo's protests and not even breaking stride as she handed out the instructions.

'Oh, I don't need to be walked home, it's not far,' Orla said.

Carrie fixed her with a look that said she was not to be argued with and Orla snapped her mouth closed.

'No problem,' Shay said.

Within seconds Carrie had frogmarched Theo out of the door and bundled him in the car.

'It really did look bad,' Fern said. 'I'm pretty sure I could see a rib.'

'He did it while we were surfing, landed badly on a rock. He wasn't fussed about it at the time, just got back on his board and carried on surfing. It was only when we got out the sea, we noticed how bad it was. He said it didn't even hurt, but you know what Theo's like,' Shay said, as he emptied pasta into a pan, filled it with water and put in on the hob.

'Theo is always getting into scrapes, breaking bones, injuring himself, he has no fear,' Fern said.

Shay retrieved the garlic bread from the fridge, placed it on a baking tray and popped it in the oven. It was weird seeing him so domesticated after seeing him in the park, smoking and drinking with his mates, playing music, being cool and aloof. This was a whole other side to him. He must have only been a year or two older than her and Fern, maybe fifteen or sixteen at most. Most of the kids her age could make themselves some toast if need be and while heating some garlic bread and cooking some pasta was hardly cordon bleu, she liked that he was capable. She had taught herself to cook as a distraction from what was going on in the house and she loved the escape it gave her. Measuring and mixing ingredients together and experimenting with different flavours was very cathartic.

'Can I help with anything?' Orla offered.

'No, it's all in hand. Mum's already made the meatballs and the sauce,' Shay said as Fern laid the table.

Within a few minutes dinner was served and it tasted delicious. Home-cooked meals seemed to be a thing of the past now. Her parents were too bitter and angry to want to cook for each other. Her dad would go out a lot and her mum didn't want to be seen to be at home waiting for him and would go out too. Orla relished those times when there was silence in the house. That's when she would cook for herself but having someone else cook for her was a rare treat.

Fern chatted happily all the way through dinner and Shay barely said a word, but no sooner had the last mouthful been eaten than there was a knock on the door.

'That's my ride,' Fern said, cheerfully. 'I'll see you tomorrow, Orla.'

Fern grabbed her bag and ran out the front door, leaving Orla and Shay alone.

Shay started loading everything into the dishwasher and she gave him a hand clearing the table.

'I'll walk you home,' Shay said, once that was done.

'You don't have to do that.'

'Oh, I do. Mum would kill me if I didn't.'

'But I was just going to hang out on the beach for a bit.'

'It's a bit cold for that isn't it?'

'My coat is pretty warm and I have a hat and gloves in my bag.'

'Are you meeting friends?'

'No, I go by myself.'

'Then I'll come with you.'

'You really don't have to do that, I'm sure you have better things to do with your time.'

'No, I really don't. I'm going to walk you home, no matter what time that is.'

She folded her arms across her chest, not sure she was keen on the idea of a self-imposed babysitter.

He mirrored her actions and she let out a huff of annoyance. 'Fine. Come with me to the beach. I warn you, it's very boring. I just sit there and look out at the sea.'

'I'm pretty sure I'm capable of doing that too.'

He ushered her out the back door, grabbed his jacket and locked the door behind them. 'Which beach?'

'Cranberry Cove.' She waited to see if he baulked at the idea – it was the furthest away.

'We'll take my bike then.'

He wandered off to the garage at the side, unlocked it and wheeled out a bike. It looked like something that was cross between a motorbike and a bicycle. It had pedals and a chain around the back wheel, but it had large thick, off-road tyres, chopper style handles and a double-length seat that could easily fit two people.

'That looks like a pretty cool bike.'

'It's electric. I persuaded Mum to buy it off eBay for a tenner. It didn't work so I replaced all the parts, replaced the tyres and the suspension, fitted a new seat, spray painted it, spent many a loving hour doing it up. She's my pride and joy.' He swung his leg over the seat. 'Come on, hop on.'

'What?'

'Get on.'

She stared at him.

'You want to get to the beach some time tonight, right?'

She sighed. Her peaceful evening was definitely taking a weird turn. She climbed on the bike behind him. She looked around for something to hold onto, but he took her hands and wrapped them around his waist. She couldn't help but notice his rock-hard stomach.

'Is this how you get the girls, impress them with your flashy bike and then give them rides around the town?'

He burst out laughing and she loved the sound of it. 'Girls don't tend to be impressed by an oversized bicycle with a top speed of twenty miles an hour. Girls who like that sort of thing, prefer real motorbikes. The double seat was for Fern. She has no qualms about riding around on the back of my slightly-less-than-cool bike.'

He started the battery and it made a high-pitched whirring noise, which made her giggle. It definitely wasn't the roar of a motorbike. But when they started moving, she was surprised by how fast it seemed and how exhilarating it was to be driving over the cliff tops. The sun had already set but it was that beautiful twilight time of day where the sky was still pink above the sea. She held him tighter and couldn't help letting out a little whoop of excitement, which made him laugh.

It only took a few minutes to reach the top of Cranberry Cove. The tide was In tonight so the public path to the beach would be no good.

'How are you planning on getting down?' Shay asked.

'I have my ways. Can you head to Starlight Cottage?'

He rode the bike in that direction and then stopped

outside, killing the engine. The house was in darkness and there was no car in the drive or any sign anyone was staying there.

They climbed off and she gestured for him to follow her around the back. He wheeled his bike into the back garden and stashed it against the fence so it was hidden from the main road.

'Isn't this trespassing?' Shay said.

'We have to live a little dangerously. Besides this house is rarely in use. It's a holiday let with its own indoor pool. It's such a shame that it's not lived in and loved. It's such a beautiful house. One day, I'm going to live here and treat it with the love it deserves.'

'I like that dream.'

She led the way to the steps at the back of the garden and followed them down to the beach.

There wasn't anyone else down there – there never was – so she found a place at the back of the beach and sat down. He sat down next to her. She wondered if he would talk but he didn't, so she just enjoyed the silence, watching the waves gently rolling in. She could sit like this forever and never get bored of it.

She took a flask of hot chocolate from her bag, poured it into a mug and passed it to Shay. He thanked her. She poured some out for her in the cup shaped lid of the flask and took a sip.

After a while he spoke. 'Do you mind if I smoke?'

'I'd rather you didn't,' Orla said.

He shrugged. 'OK.'

She felt bad. He was being kind enough to accompany

her, if he wanted to smoke then he should be allowed to smoke.

'Sorry, I just hate the smell. Dad used to smoke when I was little but he quit years ago. Now he's started up again and I'm pretty sure he does it just to piss my mum off. They row so often about it and he seems to do it even more, smoking three or four in quick succession while she screams at him the whole time. Now the smell just reminds me of anger and hatred and bitterness.'

'It's not a problem. It's a disgusting, unhealthy habit anyway. Not quite sure why I do it.'

'To fit in,' Orla said.

'Probably.' He looked out over the sea. 'I've spent my life desperate to be liked, to be loved and then Carrie adopts me, brings me here and it feels like a fresh start. And I just want to make friends. Being moved around so much in foster care meant I never had any friends growing up, being quiet and withdrawn also doesn't help. So now I smoke and drink because that's what the cool kids do. I listen to music I don't even like. I'm not even sure I recognise the person I'm becoming.'

Her heart went out to him. She couldn't even begin to imagine what growing up in foster care was like, being shipped from home to home, never making connections, no one really caring about him. It must have been devastating.

'I get it, I really do. But from what I've seen you're pretty cool in your own right and if you did the things *you* like to do, you'd find your own people. Real friends that like you for who you are.'

'Someone like you?'

She smiled. 'We can be friends.'

'But only if I stop smoking.'

'Oh no, I'd never ask you to change anything about you for me. And I don't care if you smoke or not, I'd just prefer you don't do it around me.'

'I can do that. So you've never felt the need to fit in?'

'I don't know. I like people, I like having friends like Fern and you and others. But I also just really like being on my own too. Maybe it's that only child syndrome, you learn to keep yourself occupied, depend on yourself and no one else. I moved schools when I was younger, no idea why, I don't think my parents liked the teachers. I was bullied quite badly at the new school for being the new kid. It didn't make me want to fit in with them, it made me want to be alone. I like to read so I'd always try to find a quiet spot at lunch or breaktime to read a book. A book never lets you down, it never calls you names, it never tries to hurt you.'

He nodded. 'Yeah, I get that. And I bet it feels like your parents have let you down too?'

'Oh yeah, and I feel quite angry about that. When they're both at home they fight, constantly. When it's just one of them they bitch about the other one to me and then get annoyed when I don't take their side. My mum isn't even speaking to me right now because I didn't agree with her over some petty thing she was berating my dad over.'

'What's their deal, why do they hate each other so much?'

'Dad had an affair. I think it caught my mum completely off guard, she had no idea. She always said they were happy. I remember us all being happy together but clearly my dad wasn't. And it wasn't even a one-time only thing, it had been going on for two years before he was found out. Dad was hugely apologetic, swore it would never happen again, said it didn't mean anything, the usual cliches. Mum was heartbroken, I was too if truth be told. Anyway, Dad insisted we moved away, start over. I think that was partly because we lived in a small village and everyone hated him for what he had done to my mum. But we moved here, left behind all our friends and family and then he had another affair so now my mum hates him even more. And I just wish they would get a divorce, move out, and move on with their lives or at least move out and hate each other from a distance, but they prefer shouting and screaming at each other. They seem to get some perverse enjoyment out of it. This is why I come here to get away from them. And I suppose there's a tiny part of me that would like them to look around one day and think: where's Orla? But I don't think that will ever happen.'

'That sounds rough.'

'Yeah it is. As soon as I'm eighteen, I'm going to go to university and get away from here. But that's another four years.'

'You know you'd always be welcome to stay at ours. We have a spare bedroom that's never used. Carrie would welcome you with open arms. I know it's not a permanent fix unless you can persuade Carrie to adopt you too, but at least it would give you a break a few nights a week.'

Orla thought about how blissful it would be to not be woken every morning with fighting and shouting. 'You know, I might take you up on that. I'm honestly dreading Christmas this year and normally it's my favourite time of year. We haven't even decorated the house yet, and I love decorating the tree. I doubt there will even be a tree this year, so yes, having a night or two away from the hell would be wonderful, if Carrie really is OK with it.'

'I know she'd be OK with it, she's that sort of person. Let me have a word with her.'

'Thank you. I mean, you don't even know me.'

He shrugged. 'We're friends, right?'

She grinned. She liked that. 'So you know my story, what's yours? You said you know what it's like to be in the middle of a toxic relationship.'

Shay let out a heavy sigh. 'Greg, the man that biologically is my father, used to beat my mum, pretty much every day.'

Her heart dropped. 'Oh Shay, I'm so sorry.'

'Yeah, it was horrible. I still have nightmares about it, I can still hear the sound of his fist making contact with her. My mum adored him, she would always say it was her fault, that she deserved to be hit. I always tried to stop him and he hit me a few times when I got in the way but he never laid into me like he did with my mum. Generally, he would just shove me aside and I was too weak and too small to stop him.'

He swallowed and she took his hand, although he didn't seem to notice.

'The dad of one of my friends at school was a police officer and when I told my friend what was happening, he said you have to get evidence, that his dad always said that criminals got away with stuff when there was no evidence. So I started filming it. Mum had one of those little camcorder things, and I filmed him hitting her, over several different nights. Then one night, when it was particularly bad, after he'd shoved me into a wall when I tried to stop him, I called the police. They came while he was still beating her and unfortunately for him, he was doing it in the lounge with the curtains wide open and they saw everything. That coupled with the videos I'd taken assured he went away for a long time, despite my mum refusing to press charges. They didn't need her to with that evidence.'

Orla stayed quiet, somehow knowing there was more.

'My mum hated me for what I'd done. She stopped giving me food, saying that Greg always paid for the food and now he wasn't there, I wasn't getting any. So I ended up stealing food from shops so I wouldn't starve. She would shout at me constantly, sometimes slap me. It wasn't good. Social services were soon alerted. It seems my neighbours were quite happy to turn a blind eye when it was just my dad beating my mum, but not when it was my mum beating me. They took me into emergency care when I was eight and... I never went back. My mum made it very clear she didn't want me and there were no other relatives, so I stayed in foster care for the next five years.'

'Shay I'm so sorry you went through that, it sounds horrific.'

He shrugged. 'It wasn't the best start in life.'

'I get why you're quiet and withdrawn now and the need to be loved,' she stroked his hand and he looked down, suddenly realising his hand was wrapped in hers. She quickly snatched it away, but he caught it and held it in his again as he stared out to sea.

'I think I've spoken more to you tonight than anyone else I've met since I've been here. I've told you things I've barely told anyone,' Shay said, shaking his head.

'Well, as the old advert says, 'It's good to talk.'

He smiled. 'Yeah, it is. To the right people.'

They sat in silence for a while as the last of the daylight faded away and the stars peppered the night sky, but he didn't let go of her hand.

Eventually he looked at his watch. 'I should probably get you home.'

She looked at her watch and realised it was ten o'clock. Carrie would be wondering where Shay was even if her own parents didn't care.

She nodded and still holding her hand, he stood up and then led the way back up the stairs. He grabbed his bike, wheeled it back out onto the road and swung his leg over it. She climbed on behind him, holding him tight. He didn't go over the cliff tops this time, he stuck to the road, which was a slightly longer way back, but probably safer and then rode into the town to get to her house. He pulled up outside and killed the engine. Surprisingly, there was silence from inside the house.

31

'Thank you for tonight,' Orla said, climbing off the back.

'My pleasure and I'll speak to Carrie about you staying.'

'Thank you.'

He hesitated and she wondered, quite bizarrely, if he was thinking about giving her a kiss goodnight, but he simply nodded and drove off.

She watched him go and thought she might just have fallen a little bit in love with Shay Lucas.

CHAPTER THREE

Orla, aged 14. December 9th

Orla was sitting on the beach the next night when she heard the noise of someone carrying something down the steps from Starlight Cottage. It sounded like someone was dragging a body. She really hoped she wasn't going to be witness to a horrible crime and then she remembered she lived in Apple Hill Bay. The worst crime that happened here was kids accidentally breaking a window with a football.

Just then Shay appeared and although she knew he wouldn't be dragging a body with him, he was definitely dragging something that was big enough to be a body.

He dragged it closer to where she was sitting and she realised it was a Christmas tree.

'Shay, what are you doing?'

'You said you were going to miss decorating the tree this year, so I thought we could do it together.'

She smiled, her heart filling with love for him.

'I can't believe you brought a tree down a hundred and thirteen steps just for me. It's not even a small one.'

'Well, if we're going to do it, we should do it right.' He ripped open the netting surrounding the tree. He pulled a large bag off his shoulder, removed a tree base and slotted the Christmas tree inside, so the tree stood up, at least six or seven foot tall. He pulled out a big bag of baubles. 'My mum has thousands of baubles, as she has a different colour tree each year, last year it was gold, the year before it was red, this year it's pink. So she said I could take these blue and purple ones. I figured these ones would suit you best,' he gestured to her purple boots.

'Thank you, this is really thoughtful, and purple is my favourite colour.'

She selected a purple glittery bauble that looked like it had peacock feathers printed on the sides and hung it on the tree.

'I even brought solar-powered lights so we can leave it down here on the beach and we'll have a little bit of Christmas joy every time we come here.'

'Don't we run the risk of having it stolen if we leave it here?'

'I don't think anyone is going to be able to drag a seven-foot tree up all those steps; it was hard enough bringing it down, and the school kids tend to hang out on Blackberry Beach, not Cranberry Cove, so it will probably be quite safe, but we can always hide it at the back in one of the caves when we leave.'

'Good idea.'

Shay selected a bluey green bauble and hung it on the tree. 'What is it you love about decorating a tree?'

'I don't know, I suppose it's just that cosy family time together. Mum would always make mugs of hot chocolate with lashings of cream and marshmallows. Dad would make paper chains that would fall apart every time he lifted it to go on the tree. They would always dance together to some cheesy Christmas song. They were so in love, so happy. I have so many memories like that, not just at Christmas but lots of other times throughout the year where we were this tight, little happy family. And now they can't even stand to be in the same room as each other. I suppose it's just that nostalgia for happier, simpler times.'

'So I guess this isn't really ticking that box for you, in that regard.'

'I don't know, I think I will always remember the year my friend dragged a Christmas tree down to the beach for me to decorate. Maybe this is about making new memories.'

He smiled at that. 'I'm a big fan of that. The first time I ever decorated a tree was the first year that Carrie fostered me. I was thirteen. I don't have any Christmas memories from my birth family. I don't remember any decorations or a special day of presents or turkey. I don't know why. Maybe we celebrated it in some low-key kind of way, but I don't remember if we did. When I was in foster care, I always felt in the way at that time of year so although there were always celebrations, I didn't feel like I was a part of it.'

He hung another bauble on the tree. 'With Carrie, she made sure I was a big part of the celebrations, the decorating, the day itself. I'd been with her for around four months at this point, which I think was the longest ever foster placement. Theo's adoption had finally come through and I remember how happy he was. As we finished decorating the tree she asked if I wanted to help her decorate the tree every year and asked if she could adopt me. I was stunned that anyone could ever want me. I think that was the first time in my life I felt loved and I'm not ashamed to admit I sobbed like a baby. I never thought she'd go through with it, I kept expecting her to change her mind, but she never did. Every Christmas since then has been a happy one. Christmas for me now means something different. So I'm all about making new memories.'

'I like that we can make new memories together,' Orla said.

He smiled and nodded. 'I do too.'

She watched him as he held her gaze and she felt something shift between them, a deeper connection perhaps, or was it something more?

CHAPTER FOUR

Orla, aged 14. December 22nd

Orla stepped out of the shower and dried herself. She had spent a blissful night in Carrie's spare room. Carrie had welcomed her with open arms just as Shay had said. She'd made a big fuss of her, making sure she had everything she needed, showing her where everything was, and it had been so wonderful and quiet. Orla and Fern had spent the night watching Christmas movies and making Christmas cookies and it had all been very sweet and wholesome and it was lovely to feel so at home, more so than in her own house.

Orla was already wondering how many times she could sleep over without overstaying her welcome. Would two nights in a row be too much? It was Christmas in a few days, could she somehow wrangle an invite to spend the day with them instead? It had been several years since she'd had a proper family Christmas and she'd missed that.

There had been no sign of Shay and Theo the night before. Fern said they were out with friends. And of course, it didn't matter except her stupid heart had really wanted to see Shay. Which was ridiculous. He had no interest in her, not romantically anyway. She'd see him with his friends in the park after school, girls hanging off him like limpets clinging to the rocks on the beach. She'd seen him kiss one or two of them too. He'd never done that with her.

It had been two weeks since that first night on the beach and he'd turned up at Cranberry Cove several times since then – sometimes they'd talk all night, sometimes they'd just sit in silence. She didn't have to try hard with Shay, she could just be herself. It was easy with him and she liked that. But he'd never kissed her like he'd done with the limpets.

Not that she cared of course. She wasn't interested in having a boyfriend. The boys at school were stupid and she'd seen enough of her parents' toxic relationship to not want that. But that didn't stop her stupid heart racing every time he appeared on the beach to spend time with her.

She wrapped a towel around her and started brushing out her wet hair, which was always a tangle of red curls after she'd washed it.

Just then the bathroom door opened and Shay walked in just wearing his pyjama bottoms.

She let out a yelp and his eyes widened in shock before he quickly clamped a hand over his eyes and turned away.

'Shit, I'm so sorry. Why didn't you lock it?'

'I thought I did. Why didn't you knock?'

'Sorry, I'm not used to knocking. Fern and Mum both have ensuite bathrooms. This is the one I share with Theo. And as unpleasant as it is, I've seen his naked ass far too many times to count.'

She laughed and looked down at herself, the towel was covering everything down to her knees. 'I'm covered up anyway, nothing to see here apart from some shoulders and I don't think they're that offensive.'

He peeped through a crack in his fingers and then dropped his hand. 'I really am sorry.'

'No need to be, no harm done. And I'm done in here, so the bathroom's yours.'

He stepped back to let her past, but he was so big she had to turn sideways to get through the doorway. His chest really was a thing of beauty, all hard and muscular, although she tried really hard not to look at it as she sidled past. She noticed he was wearing Christmassy pyjama bottoms, which no doubt Carrie had bought him, and she found that really cute and endearing.

Suddenly he put a hand out to stop her, catching her wrist in his hand. 'What's this?'

She looked at what he was pointing out and realised he was referring to the large gash on her shoulder. It had happened a few days before and was now turning an ugly purple and yellow, making it look a lot worse than it was.

She flushed. 'It's nothing.'

'It looks a lot more than nothing.'

'It was just an accident, nothing to worry about.'

'Orla,' Shay said, in a tone that said he wasn't going to be fobbed off.

'Fine. My mum threw a plate against the wall and it smashed, a bit flew off and hit me in the shoulder as I walked into the kitchen. It was an accident.'

His face darkened and she could tell he was furious. 'Do you know how many times I heard that when I was little. 'It was an accident; he didn't mean to hit me.'

'Well, it was, she wasn't aiming at me, she wasn't even aiming at my dad, he was on the opposite side of the room, she just likes to take her temper out on the plates, cups and glasses. She was very apologetic.'

'So she should be.'

'It's just a scratch.'

'Christ, Orla, a few inches higher it could have been your throat or even your eye. This isn't acceptable.'

'It's OK. I'm OK. I've done worse falling off my bike.'

He looked away and she could see he was still angry.

She decided to change the subject. 'Will I see you at the beach tonight?'

He shook his head. 'I have something I need to do.'

She nodded and stepped out of the bathroom and before she could say another word, he closed the door.

As it happened, it was raining heavily that night and while she didn't mind going to the beach in the rain, outside it looked like a monsoon so she'd decided to stay in. She was sitting in her room staring out the window while the shouting continued below her, when a taxi pulled up outside. She frowned. The house sat on its own at the top of the hill and they never got any visitors – who would want to spend an evening in this war zone? She peered through the darkness and rain and her heart leapt because the man that was struggling to drag something big out of the back of the taxi looked very much like Shay. She watched him in confusion because the thing he had pulled from the back looked like a punch bag. Then realisation hit her.

'No, no, no.'

She wasn't even dressed, she'd changed into her pyjamas a while ago with the intention to read in bed so she quickly got changed into some clothes and threw her shoes on with the hope she could reach him before he reached the house, but as she ran downstairs, Shay was struggling in through the front door with the punch bag, her bemused mum standing there watching him in confusion. There was no sign of her dad.

'What the hell is this?' her mum asked.

'It's for you Mrs Kennedy,' Shay said. 'It used to be mine, but I don't use it anymore, I bought you some boxing gloves as well, they might be a bit big but you can tighten them with these strings.'

'I don't understand,' her mum said.

Shay suddenly noticed Orla and for a second he stared at her, his eyes filled with anger and fire. She shook her head, but he turned away from her and didn't acknowledge her after that.

'Well, I hear you have quite the temper, I hear that many a plate or glass has been sacrificed in the rows with your husband. I figured if you're angry you could take it out on this instead.'

Her mum's face flushed and she looked at Orla accusingly. 'So you've made me out to be some kind of psychopath to your little friends. I don't suppose you mentioned your father's role in all of this.'

'Hey,' Shay snapped. 'Don't you dare blame her for this. Don't you fucking dare.'

Her mum paled and took a step back.

'Shay,' Orla said, coming down the last few steps. 'It's OK.'

He looked at her and then turned his attention back to her mum.

'How dare you come into my house and—'

'How dare I? How dare you treat your daughter so badly.'

Orla's dad appeared in the kitchen doorway. 'What's going on?'

'Both of you should be ashamed of yourselves,' Shay said. 'You're so righteous in your anger, so caught up in hating each other that you haven't given a single thought to how this is impacting Orla. Did you know she goes to the beach every night just so she doesn't have to be here, because being alone on the beach in the cold and dark is infinitely better than being here listening to you screaming, shouting and throwing plates at each other. Did you know that she spent the night at my house last night because she didn't want to be woken up by your endless rows yet again? You're driving your daughter away and neither of you have noticed or cared. And what about what happened the other night, when that bit of broken plate sliced open her shoulder? What if that had been a vein in her neck, what if it had been her face or her eye?'

'It was an accident,' her mum said, embarrassed.

'Well, it ends here. I don't care if you hate each other, I don't care if you really want to spend all your time shouting and screaming at each other, but you won't throw plates or cups or anything else again. You get that angry, you punch or kick the shit out of this thing. I don't want to see her get hurt again and if she does, you'll have me to answer to.'

'Are you threatening my wife?' her dad said in a rare sign of solidarity. He moved towards Shay and Shay just looked at him. At sixteen he already towered over her dad.

'Oh, like you care,' her mum snapped.

Shay rolled his eyes and moved back towards Orla, taking her hand. 'She'll be staying at mine tonight and every night until you two grow up and start acting like parents rather than toddlers throwing a tantrum.'

With that he marched out of the house, dragging Orla with him. He bundled her into the taxi and sat next to her.

'We're going back to my house,' Shay said to the taxi driver, then he sat back and stared out the window, anger rolling off him in waves.

She didn't know what to say. She couldn't help thinking he'd just made things worse. Where her mum had barely been speaking to her before, now she would be furious that she'd told Shay and that he'd embarrassed her in this way.

She didn't know whether to be angry at him. She didn't need him to fight her battles for her – she was quite capable of fighting them on her own. Except she hadn't. She should have confronted her parents long before now, but instead she'd run away and hid from her problems rather than face them head on. Even after she'd hurt her shoulder, she hadn't been brave enough to tell them enough was enough. Nothing was ever going to change unless she stood up to them and she'd had no plan of doing that. Maybe it needed someone like Shay to talk to them. Although the way he'd done it probably needed a little more finesse.

'I'm sorry. I shouldn't have done that,' Shay said. 'I've spent most of my life bitter and angry, angry at my parents, angry at the world. Carrie bought me that punch bag and she said that it was OK to be angry about the card that life has dealt me, but it was never OK to take that anger out on other people, no matter how much they pissed me off and she encouraged me to use the bag instead. In my head, I was going to give a very calm speech to your parents, very similar to the one that Carrie gave me when she bought it for me. But all that went out the window when I saw you and when your mum tried to blame you. I feel so damned protective over you.'

Her heart filled with love for him.

'How you spoke to my mum was not acceptable,' Orla said.

'No, it wasn't and I will apologise tomorrow. But I

stand by the spirit of the message. They should not be taking it out on you or putting you at risk and they need to think about how their actions impact on you.'

She leaned up and kissed him on the cheek. 'Thank you.'

He stared at her.

'No one has ever stood up for me before,' she said. 'No one has done something like that for me before.'

'I don't think you should be thanking me for that.'

'You were looking out for me and you were right and it needed to be said. Although perhaps more delicately.'

He shook his head. 'I'm not delicate, Orla, far from it. But I'm not as angry as I used to be anymore, not since Carrie adopted me. A lot of that went away. I haven't used that punch bag for over a year now. And I'm working on the rest, I promise you that.' He paused. 'I'm not my dad.'

Her heart broke for him.

'You will never be your dad. You don't need to worry about that. You're kind, caring—'

'Aggressive.'

'No, that's not who you are.'

He shook his head.

The taxi pulled up outside Shay's house. He paid and still holding her hand he led her inside.

Carrie was waiting for them in the kitchen.

'Hello Orla dear, I hear you're staying with us tonight.'

Orla bit her lip; she didn't know if she could face her parents' wrath over what just happened. She needed them to calm down first. 'If that's OK.'

'Of course it is, you are welcome here anytime. Shay

told me how you had got hurt the other night. I'm so sorry your parents' arguments have escalated to the point where you don't even feel safe in your own home.' Her eyes moved to Shay. 'Orla's parents just called, they told me what you said.'

'I'm so sorry, Mum. I just...'

Carrie put a hand up to stop him talking. 'I told them you were hot-headed and impetuous, but I could never be angry at you for sticking up for someone. I told them your delivery needed work, but you were right, their behaviour needs to stop before someone gets seriously hurt. I told them that it's none of our business if they hate each other and why but there is a third person in their relationship they have to consider. They were a lot more amicable by the time I'd finished our conversation, but I think I just echoed most of what you'd said, maybe in a more calm way.'

'I really am sorry, I didn't mean to get quite so angry. Fighting fire with fire is not the way.'

Carrie came over and gave him a big hug and Orla watched as Shay hugged her back.

'You did a good thing and I'm not going to say don't do it again, because I know you'll always protect those that need it, but maybe next time, you write down what you want to say first, or take a breath.'

'I will and I'm going to apologise to them tomorrow.'

'They want to see you both actually, tomorrow when everyone calms down. I can come with you if you want, although I think you're more than capable of handling it on your own.'

'That's OK, I'll talk to them,' Shay said.

'And I will too,' Orla said. 'It's high time that I confront them about this, it has to stop.'

Shay nodded. 'I'm going to bed,' he turned to Orla. 'Are you OK?'

'Of course.'

He gave her hand a squeeze and walked out looking like he was carrying the weight of the world on his shoulders.

Orla turned her attention to Carrie, who was watching her carefully. 'I, umm, didn't get a chance to grab any stuff, do you have a t-shirt or something I could borrow to sleep in?'

Carrie moved to a laundry basket and grabbed a t-shirt that was huge enough that it had to be Theo's or Shay's.

'It is clean, I just haven't got around to putting it back in Shay's room yet,' Carrie handed it to her.

'Thank you.'

'And there's a spare toothbrush underneath the bathroom sink.'

Orla nodded.

'Honey, don't let his... bravado scare you away.'

'I'm not scared of him, far from it.'

'Underneath all that grumpiness is a very warmhearted, lovely boy.'

'I know, he's been nothing but kind to me. I know all about his past, about what happened with his dad then his mum. I know that must have left some scars.'

Carrie looked surprised. 'It's not something he ever talks about, not even with Theo or Fern. I know of course, it was part of his case history when I first fostered him and we've talked about it briefly from time to time, but he doesn't like to discuss it, so it's nice that he feels he can share that with you. I worry that he's getting mixed up with a bad crowd but the fact he has you gives me hope.'

'Oh, we're not together,' Orla said. 'Just friends.'

'More's the pity. I think you could be very good for him. Shay blames himself for what happened to his mum, he feels he should have done more to stop it. But what could he have done? He was a little boy. But I think it's just made him so protective, especially when he sees it happening again, even if what happened to your shoulder was accidental.'

'I get that.'

Orla wondered if she should tell Carrie that probably Shay's biggest fear was that he would turn out like his dad, but it felt disloyal to discuss what he'd said behind his back. Besides, Orla knew that wasn't going to happen. He might get a bit angry, he might even get into a few fights at school, but that was very different to what his dad did. She trusted him completely. And maybe she needed to tell him that.

'I'm going to go to bed too,' Orla said.

Carrie nodded.

'Thank you for letting me stay.'

'You're always welcome here.'

Orla went down the hall and stopped outside Shay's bedroom door. After a moment, she knocked on the door and he opened it.

'Are you OK?' she asked.

He nodded.

'Stop beating yourself up, you were trying to do something good. OK, you swore at my mum, and you got angry, but you didn't get violent. That's not you. You're a good man and I trust you.'

He studied her.

'Can I give you a hug?'

He blinked in surprise and then he nodded. She slid her arms around him and after a moment he wrapped himself around her, holding her tight.

'Thank you,' he muttered roughly into the top of her head.

She pulled back to look at him. 'I'll always be here for you.'

'And I'll always be here for you,' he said.

She smiled and stepped back. 'I'll see you tomorrow.'

With that she went into the bedroom and when she turned to close the door behind her, he was still standing there, watching her go.

CHAPTER FIVE

Orla, aged 14. December 23rd

It was just starting to snow as Orla and Shay walked towards her house the next day. Orla loved snow. They didn't get too much of it in Ireland and even less of it now she was living on the south coast of England, so it was even more special when it did snow.

'I love it when it snows. There's something magical about it,' Orla said, catching a snowflake in the palm of her hand. When I was a kid, I used to love making snowmen or snow angels.'

'Snow angels?'

'You know, when you lie on your back and move your arms and legs to make the imprint of an angel in the snow.'

'Ah yes, I've seen people do that in the cheesy Christmas movies that Fern loves so much.'

'You never made snow angels?' Orla asked and then cursed herself. Of course he hadn't. Nothing about his childhood was normal. His birth parents would never have done something like that with him. 'Sorry, that was a stupid question.'

'You don't need to apologise.'

'I do, that was insensitive.'

'You're fine. I don't think my life is any worse off because I didn't make snow angels. My parents were the worst but not making snow angels with me is the lesser of their crimes.'

Orla smiled sadly. 'You know, I think you're pretty amazing.'

'Why?'

'You're so resilient and strong. Life dealt you a really crappy hand and you bounce back.'

'Oh, that's all Carrie, not me. She did that. Finally being loved by someone, well three people actually, helped to heal a lot of wounds.'

'But it takes courage and determination to want to make that change rather than letting the bitterness and anger eat away at you.'

'There's still some anger in there.'

'Of course there is, but you know how to deal with it. As you said, you haven't used that punchbag for over a year.'

Shay was silent and she hoped he was taking it on

board. He wasn't the sort of person that took compliments very easily.

They started walking up Orla's garden path to her house and he let out a sigh. She took his hand. She knew he was nervous about facing her parents again. He'd even brought her mum a bunch of flowers to apologise, which Orla secretly thought was probably overkill considering her mum's behaviour recently.

Orla let herself into the kitchen, pulling Shay behind her.

'Hello!' she called out to her parents and after a few moments they appeared in the doorway.

'Hello Orla honey, it's good to see you,' her mum said, sweetly, which was definitely not like the way she'd spoken to her over the last few months. But Orla realised that her mum was as nervous as Shay was.

Shay cleared his throat. 'Mrs Kennedy, I wanted to apologise for the way I spoke to you yesterday.' He offered out the flowers. 'I stand by what I said, I don't want Orla to get hurt, but I should not have spoken to you in that manner.'

'Shay, I'm glad you did. It gave us the kick up the bum we needed,' her mum gestured for them to sit and they all sat down at the kitchen table. 'We have been so blind to what we were doing to you, Orla, every day we'd scream and shout at each other and neither of us thought about how that affected you and I'm so sorry about that.'

'It's been unbearable,' Orla said. 'I never wanted to come home.'

'Your mum's right,' said her dad, 'we were selfish, only

thinking about ourselves and while we have our disagreements, we both still love you.'

'I felt like I was stuck in the middle,' Orla said. 'Both of you wanting me to take your side and then if I didn't, you'd get all arsey with me. It wasn't fair.'

'No it wasn't. Our argument has nothing to do with you and we shouldn't have put you in that position,' her dad said, and her mum narrowed her eyes slightly at him, as if she thought he was putting the blame on her. Although that part had been mainly her mum – she had refused to talk to Orla for the last few weeks because she hadn't taken her mum's side.

'We talked a lot last night,' Orla's mum said. 'Well, we argued and then we talked. We don't want to drive you from your own home. Your dad is going to move into the annexe so we have some space from each other. We'd obviously done that up to start renting it out as a holiday let but this is more important. I can't promise there won't be any more arguments, but I categorically promise that there won't be any more plates or glasses getting thrown. I'm going to take Shay's advice and use the punchbag if I get that angry, but I think having some space from each other will really help.'

Her heart sank a little. She'd kind of hoped they were going to go ahead with a divorce. There was never any coming back from this; her dad had an affair twice, her mum could never trust him again and the screaming and shouting proved they hated each other – what was the point of prolonging it? Did they really think that her dad living five metres away from their back door was going to make a difference? But she wasn't the adult in this relationship so she certainly didn't feel like she could beg them for a divorce instead.

'I just want to come home and not hear you screaming at each other.'

'We're going to do our very best,' her dad said.

'And as tomorrow is Christmas Eve, I thought we could decorate the tree together, in the lounge, just you and me,' her mum said.

'And when you're finished you can help me decorate the annexe, put your festive touch on it,' her dad said.

Orla felt a little sad about that. Although she couldn't think of anything worse than decorating a tree with the three of them together as it was bound to lead to more arguments, it felt sad that big events like Christmas and birthdays would have to be so divided and separate going forward. She missed the life they had before her dad had an affair. Christmas had always been a wonderful day with her family. There was never any going back to that.

'And for Christmas Day we thought—' her mum started.

'Orla is coming to mine for Christmas Day lunch,' Shay said.

She looked at him. That was news to her, although she had mentioned to Shay how she was dreading Christmas day this year. Suddenly she couldn't think of anything she wanted more.

'That's right, I didn't want to spend Christmas here and Shay offered.'

'Well that works out fine,' her dad said. 'You can spend

Christmas morning with your mum, lunch with Shay and the afternoon with me.'

Orla nodded. It was nice they were trying to make an effort.

'And despite last night, we're glad you have someone fighting your corner, like we should have. We didn't even know you were dating anyone,' her mum said.

'We're not dating,' Shay was quick to correct her. 'If she was dating someone, I'm sure she would choose someone a hell of a lot better than me. We're just friends and it won't ever be anything more than that, so you don't need to worry.'

Orla chewed on her thumbnail as a little bit of her died inside.

CHAPTER SIX

Orla, aged 14. Christmas Day

Orla walked towards Shay's house and smiled up at the snow as it fell heavily from the sky. It was evening on Christmas Day and Apple Hill Bay was enjoying the first white Christmas in twenty-three years, or so the news said. It had been a lovely day and not because of the awkwardness of both her parents trying to make the day as happy as possible, although she did appreciate them trying. But lunch with Shay and his family had been perfect. The food had been delicious, there'd been laughter and chatting, they'd played games and it felt wonderful to part of a happy, family Christmas again. She had missed it and she hadn't realised how much.

The snow had fallen quite heavily over the last few

hours and it was now almost a foot deep in the drifts that hugged the edges of the roads. So Orla had a plan.

She walked up to the farmhouse and she could see through the windows that Carrie had fallen asleep on the sofa and Fern was fast asleep with her head in her mum's lap. She walked round the outside of the building until she found Shay's room. He was lying on his bed, reading a book.

She tapped on the window and he looked up in surprise, then she watched the smile fill his face as he saw her. He hurried over and opened the window.

'Orla, are you OK? What are you doing here? Aren't you supposed to be with your dad?'

'I was for a few hours, now he's gone out with friends and it's snowing, and I thought I'd come back over and teach you how to do a snow angel.'

His eyebrows lifted in surprise and then he smiled. 'You want me to lie on the wet floor and wave my arms and legs around?'

'Trust me, it's fun. Besides, everyone should get to make snow angels at least once in their life.'

'OK, yes, you're right, I can see my whole life has been empty without it,' he said dryly. He grabbed his coat and hat, shoved his feet in his boots and climbed out the window. 'Right where do you want me?'

'We have to find an area of relatively undisturbed snow,' she looked around. 'Over there should do it.' They walked over to the back of the garden and Orla lay down in the snow and for a moment she just enjoyed staring up at the snowflakes as they gently swirled above them. Shay lay down in the snow next to her.

'What's next in my education?'

'Just move your arms and legs like you're doing jumping jacks, like this.' She started sliding her arms up and down across the ground, spraying herself with snow as she did it. She started laughing and to her surprise, Shay, who was clearly doing this under duress, started laughing too.

They lay there looking up at the snow falling above them laughing at the silliness of making snow angels.

He rolled onto his side to look at her and she did too.

'You're right, that was fun,' Shay said, sweeping a soggy strand of hair from her face. The smile fell from his face as he looked at her and his eyes cast down to her lips.

Oh god, he was going to kiss her. Her heart soared. She leaned closer.

He cleared his throat and sat up. 'I have a present for you actually. I didn't want to give it earlier as I didn't want the others to see. Come on, you should have it while it's still Christmas.'

He hopped up and her heart sank with disappointment. He reached out a hand and helped her up.

'They look pretty cool,' Shay said, gesturing to the snow angels Orla had almost completely forgotten about.

He gestured to the window and she climbed through, then he followed her.

'I got you a present too,' Orla said, fishing in her coat pocket for the box. 'Why don't you open that first.' She thrust the box towards him, hoping that she'd got this right.

'You didn't have to get me something.'

'Of course I did.'

He opened the box and studied the starfish necklace. She knew he wore jewellery; he had a silver circle the shape of wave on a cord around his neck so she hoped he'd like this too.

'The starfish is a symbol of resilience. Did you know when they lose an arm, they can grow another one and some starfish can grow a whole body just from one arm? I wanted to give you this as a reminder of how far you've come. Despite your terrible upbringing you're a good man and a great friend. I know we've only known each other for a few weeks but I feel very lucky to have you in my life.'

He shook his head. 'No, I'm the lucky one to have you as a friend. Thank you, this is really cool.' He immediately wrapped the black chord round his neck and fastened it. Then he leaned down and kissed her on the cheek and the feel of his lips on her skin gave her goosebumps of happiness. 'I umm... made you something,' Shay said, wiping his hands, he moved to the drawers and pulled out a box. He passed it to her.

She opened it up to see a carved wooden sun on a pale gold piece of chord. The sun was carved from the palest wood, so it was almost white and seemed to gleam under the lights.

'You made this?'

'Yeah, wood carving is a bit of a hobby for me.'

'It's beautiful.'

'It's because you are the light in my darkness. I know that's a cheesy thing to say but it's true, when I'm with you it feels like I'm stepping into the warmth of the sun.'

She stared at him. 'Shay, I...'

'And I don't want to lose you as a friend, so I'm going to do everything in my power not to cock this up. You're different to any other girl I've been with, our friendship is special and I won't compromise that.'

She didn't know what he meant by that. How could he possibly compromise their friendship? 'Shay, I'm not going anywhere.'

He nodded, brushing his hand through his hair.

'Thank you for this,' Orla took it out of the box and fastened it at the back of her neck. They stared at each other and she wondered whether it would be appropriate to give him a kiss on the cheek too. Just as she plucked up the courage to do so, he took a definite step back. She cleared her throat. 'Well, I should go, it's getting late.'

'You could stay here,' Shay said.

For a second Orla thought he was gesturing to his bed before she smiled and shook her head. Of course he wasn't, he'd backed away from kissing her and mentioned he saw her as a friend at least twice in the last minute. He obviously meant the spare room.

'I could, but Mum might be wondering where I am. She doesn't know I came out tonight.'

'I'll walk you back then.'

He climbed back out the window and helped her to do the same. He took her hand as they crunched along through the snow and it made her smile so much. It was so quiet and right then it felt as if they were the only two people in the world. She loved being with Shay, chatting to him or just quietly being together. There was something about him that made her feel so peaceful and happy.

'Have you had a good day?' Shay said.

'Yes, thank you so much for inviting me.'

'No problem, I just couldn't bear the thought of you sitting there at home alone on Christmas Day, while your parents screamed at each other. Figured you deserved a break on Christmas Day of all days.'

'Thank you. And my parents tried really hard, again thanks to you. But it was lovely spending time with your family. They're brilliant.'

'I know. I'm very lucky to have Carrie and two annoying siblings.'

Orla smiled at that. 'You love them really.'

'Yeah, I do. And I'm very lucky to have such a wonderful friend too. I'm not sure what I did to deserve you.'

'Just being a really decent bloke will do it, respectful, kind, protective. I know you don't see it, but you have great qualities. It's your resilience. Your determination to be a better person than the poor role models your parents gave you.'

He didn't say anything and she knew he didn't agree with that. She'd just have to keep telling him, one day he might believe what a wonderful man he was.

They reached her house and he walked her right up to her door. She turned to face him.

'Happy Christmas, Shay.'

He smiled and bent his head to kiss her on the cheek again. 'Merry Christmas, Orla.'

She watched him turn and go. She smiled, as despite everything that had happened with her parents, this Christmas had turned out to be one of her best.

CHAPTER SEVEN

Present day

Shay watched in horror as water poured in the passenger side, sloshing over Orla's limp, unconscious body. She was alive, she had to be – he couldn't bear the thought that she was dead. Waves pounded against the car, flipping it upside down as easily as if it was a toy car. They had to get out.

He opened the car door, undid his seatbelt and he hit the roof of the car hard. He rearranged himself, undid Orla's seatbelt and caught her before she hit the roof too. Cradling her head against his chest, he managed to manoeuvre himself backwards out of the car as it was battered against the waves.

She flopped uselessly in his arms as he dragged her out of the sea up onto the sand that was, as yet, not reached by the tide. But it was on its way in, they didn't have long. He lay her down carefully on the sand, hoping that he hadn't done more damage to her body manhandling her out of the car. She was soaked, they both were, and the snow was continuing to fall. He leaned over her and could feel her breath on the side of his face. He crumpled with relief.

He grabbed his phone from his back pocket, but it was dripping with water and not working.

He needed to call for help. He looked around desperately. The stairs up to his cottage weren't far away, but he couldn't leave her alone and he didn't want to carry her and potentially cause more injuries to her.

He shook her shoulder, trying to rouse her but she didn't stir. He stroked her face.

'Come on baby, please wake up.'

CHAPTER EIGHT

Orla, aged 16. December 18th

Orla made her way down to Cranberry Cove and smiled
to see that Shay was sitting there waiting for her.

Their Christmas tree, this year dressed in gold,
sparkled and twinkled as it sat on the beach behind him. It
had become a tradition now, every December 1st, Shay
would drag a tree down onto the beach and they would
decorate it together and she loved that they had that thing
that was just theirs.

'Hey,' she offered him a piece of Christmas pudding
fudge from her bag and he took one. She poured out two
mugs of hot chocolate from the flask she'd brought with
her. 'I have a question for you.'

'Shoot.'

'And you have to be honest.'

'I'm always honest with you.' He popped the fudge in his mouth.

'Have you had sex?'

He choked on the fudge, and she slapped him hard on the back. 'Oh my god, are you OK?'

He recovered himself and cleared his throat. 'I wasn't ready for that question, why would you want to know that?'

Orla sighed. 'It seems like everyone in the world has had sex apart from me. And it's not like I'm saving myself for marriage or the greatest love story, it's just that I'm only sixteen and the few boys I've dated I've certainly not wanted to go that far with. All the girls say sex isn't a big deal, it doesn't mean anything. And judging from their less than complimentary reviews of sex, it doesn't even seem that enjoyable, so I'm certainly not expecting it to be this beautiful, special thing that you read about in books or see in movies, but... I don't know, I just feel that the man I'm with should at least set my world on fire. I should be attracted to him. When we kiss, it should mean something.'

She stared out at the sea, feeling her cheeks flame. And that might be where the problem lay because the only man who set her world on fire was the one sitting next to her. And nothing had ever happened or would ever happen between them; they were friends and always would be. He didn't see her that way. But she knew that if they ever did kiss, at least for her, it would be electric. And she supposed she was looking for that. When she dated, when she kissed a boy, she was always looking for that excitement, that thrill that she knew she'd get from kissing Shay. She was setting herself up for failure because nothing would ever come close to how she felt for him.

'I don't think you're wrong for waiting,' Shay said. 'It has to feel right. The person has to be right. You shouldn't just have sex for the sake of having sex. And a lot of people who say they've had sex are lying simply because everyone else is saying they've had sex. I bet there are a lot more virgins in Apple Hill Bay than you think.'

'So have you?'

He paused before answering. 'Yes.'

'More than once?'

'Yes.'

'With more than one woman?'

'Not at the same time but yes, I've slept with more than one woman.'

'How many is more than one?'

'Too many, but Orla, the life I lead is not one to admire. I drink too much, smoke too much, get into too many fights and sleep with women when I don't even know their name. I've never loved any of them, barely even like them, what does that say about me? I'm seventeen, do you think I'm proud of that? I scraped through my GCSEs with no more than a handful of satisfactory grades. There will be no university for me. So don't think just because I've had sex that I should be held in some great esteem. I have a lot more admiration for you, someone who respects themselves than someone like me, a complete shitshow. Also I swear too much too. I'm clearly such a catch.'

She hated when he spoke about himself like that. 'There might not be any university for you, but you are studying a BTEC in carpentry and doing a City and Guilds in bricklaying and one in plumbing. You have already secured an apprenticeship at the White Cliff Bay furniture company for when you finish sixth form and I know how hard they are to get so don't make out like you're an uneducated lazy arse idiot. Just because you're not academic doesn't mean you're stupid. And regardless of all that other stuff you said, you're one of the kindest, loveliest men I know and that is far more important than how much you drink or how many women you've slept with.'

He looked out to sea, and she could tell he didn't believe her.

'OK, that aside. What was your first time like?'

'Quick,' Shay laughed. 'Thankfully it wasn't her first time, I'd have felt awful if it was. I think it lasted no more than thirty seconds. No woman wants to look back on their first time with that kind of disappointment. I had no idea what I was doing, or how to please a woman. Thankfully my skills have come a long way since then. Apparently, it's something I'm quite good at.'

She knew he wasn't just saying that to impress her. He never blew his own trumpet.

'So you enjoy it?'

'Most men enjoy sex because they almost always come. Women's orgasms are apparently harder to achieve.'

'Apparently?'

'Well, as I said, it's the one thing I'm good at. But sex

for me is more than just a meaningless orgasm. When I'm with these women they look at me like I'm someone special, like I'm not some worthless piece of crap, and I enjoy that feeling, no matter if it's only for one night.'

'I've never looked at you like you're worthless, I've always seen you for the man you are, not the man you love to hate. I've always thought you were special and I don't need an orgasm to think that.'

He smiled. 'Good job too, I don't think I could look myself in the eye if I slept with you.'

A stab of pain pierced her heart.

'What does that mean?'

'You deserve someone so much better than me. And that's who you should wait for, someone who will treat you with the respect, care and love that you deserve. You are one of the most incredible people I've ever met and you should be with someone incredible too. Don't jump into bed with someone just for the sake of having sex. Aim higher than that.'

'You're right, I'm not going to rush into this and I'm certainly not going to sleep with some random guy I've only known for a few hours. Are you going to Clara's Christmas party tomorrow?'

Shay nodded. 'I'm friends with her brother and Melody wants to go.'

Orla suppressed an eye roll at the mention of his latest girlfriend. She was a bit of cow, always wanted Shay to pay for everything and got super jealous if he even spoke to another girl. Orla couldn't help thinking that Shay deserved better too.

'I hate parties,' Orla said. 'It's not my sort of thing at all. Especially as I don't drink. But I like Clara and I promised I'd go. But now everyone is talking about how they're going to have sex at the party. It's a large house apparently, with lots of bedrooms. Half my friends that are going are single, but they're all excited about the prospect of hooking up with someone from the party. I can't think of anything worse. I will stand in the corner, drink orange juice and sneak out after a few hours once everyone is too drunk to notice.'

'Good plan. I'd much rather be doing that than making awkward social chit chat.'

'Is Fern going?' Orla asked, hoping she'd have at least one person on her wavelength to talk to.

'No, Mum is taking her on this painting course for the weekend. It's up in Exeter, so they're staying over tonight and tomorrow night.'

'Oh, she's been so excited about this course, I didn't realise she was staying over.'

'I think that part was kind of last minute.'

'So you and Theo have been left to your own devices?'

'No parties in the house and no overnight guests. She means Melody. Mum doesn't like her.'

'Why not?'

'She doesn't trust her. To be fair, Mum doesn't like any of the girls I date. She has very high standards of what kind of girl she wants for me. I'm more realistic. But you can stay over if you want. Mum's always happy for you to stay.'

Orla smiled. She had stayed over at least once a week

over the last few years. Despite her parents' promises, they still rowed often, although the plate throwing and glass smashing had stopped. But Carrie always made her feel welcome.

'How do you think Melody will feel if she knows that I'm staying over but she's not allowed to?'

'Well, I don't plan on telling her. She's staying over at Clara's house anyway.'

'Won't she be expecting you to stay with her?'

He pulled a face. 'I'd rather make sure you get back home safely, so come and get me when you're ready to leave.'

'You'd rather come back with me and spend the night alone in your bed, than have sex with your girlfriend.'

'Yes,' he said without hesitation.

She smiled and shook her head. She was never going to get over this man.

CHAPTER NINE

Orla, aged 16. December 19th

Orla was drunk and she was so annoyed.

She'd arrived at the party, said hello to Clara and then lurked in a corner hoping to sneak out at an appropriate time. But then Kirk had come over to talk to her. At least she thought he said his name was Kirk, he might have said Clark, she wasn't sure. And while Kirk was definitely not her type and she wasn't interested in him in that way, he was nice enough to chat to. He was charming and sweet and it beat being awkwardly alone. He kept on getting drinks for her from the kitchen which was filled with people, and she had insisted he only got her some orange juice but some of them had tasted funny. He said there was only orange and passionfruit available, and she had assumed the funny taste was the passionfruit which she'd never had, but now it was quite clear it was something else, maybe vodka or Bacardi which she'd never had either. She was so stupid. She didn't know if he'd done it deliberately or whether it had been a mistake, but she cursed herself for being so naïve.

She was so drunk now, she couldn't even stand. She couldn't see straight and she felt so tired, she felt like she could curl up on this sofa and go to sleep for a hundred years. The house was decorated in full Christmas regalia and the flashing, twinkling lights, which Orla had thought were beautiful when she arrived, were now making her head hurt, although that could easily be the alcohol that was doing that, but the lights were definitely too bright for her eyes.

Kirk was on the other side of the room chatting with his friends and they were all laughing and clapping him on the back as if he'd done something brilliant and weirdly, they all kept on looking over at her as if she was the something brilliant he'd done and none of that made sense. Nothing made sense.

She saw Shay coming towards her. He'd come over to say hello when he'd first arrived and checked in with her an hour ago before the alcohol had well and truly hit, but he'd been with Melody for most of the night and she clearly didn't like it when Shay came and spoke to Orla.

'Are you OK?' Shay asked, concern etched on his face.

'No Shay, I'm drunk, I've only been drinking orange juice all night, but I think something was in it because now my head is spinning, I can barely stand and I don't feel well.'

At least that's what she tried to say, it sounded a lot more slurred in her ears.

'OK, let's get you home,' Shay said.

Just then Melody appeared at his side. 'What's going on?'

'I'm taking Orla home.'

'Why?'

'Because she's drunk.'

'It's a party, everyone here is drunk.'

Shay ignored her and turned his attention back to Orla. 'Do you have a coat or a bag?'

She shook her head which made her brain wobble inside her head.

'Oh come on, don't go, it's only ten o'clock,' Melody whined. 'You haven't danced with me yet.'

'I don't dance.'

'But I wanted to show you the summer house in the garden. Can I show you? It will just take five minutes.'

He looked back at Orla and she really didn't want to spoil his fun. It wasn't his fault she was stupid enough to get drunk, nor was it his responsibility.

'Go, I'm OK here, I'm not going anywhere,' Orla said.

'Please, just two minutes, I promise you'll love it,' Melody said.

He nodded. 'Two minutes, then I'm taking Orla home.' He turned back to Orla. 'Stay here.'

She nodded weakly.

Melody dragged him off in the direction of the garden and Orla flopped back on the sofa. But after a few minutes there was no sign of him and she was starting to feel a bit sick. She really needed to go home and she really needed someone to help her.

She staggered to her feet and wobbled off in the direction of the garden. She felt so rough. She made it outside and while there was no sign of him, there were lights on in the summer house. She wobbled down the path and peered through the window. Shay was sitting on the sofa and Melody was straddling him, kissing him passionately. And while it shouldn't hurt as he'd had multiple girlfriends over the years, some of which he'd clearly had sex with, it still did make her heart ache when she saw him kissing someone that wasn't her, knowing it would never be her.

Melody suddenly whipped off her top to show she wasn't wearing a bra, grabbed Shay's hands and placed them over her breasts.

Orla quickly turned away. She certainly didn't want to see any more. She wobbled back to the house and as soon as she stepped inside, Kirk was waiting for her.

'Hey babe, are you OK?' he wrapped his arms round her shoulders.

'No, I'm drunk thanks to you. I said I only wanted orange juice.'

'Oh sweetheart, I'm so sorry. I had no idea, I just thought it was normal orange juice. I feel so bad.'

Orla shook her head. Maybe it had been a mistake.

'I don't feel well, I need to go home.'

'Look, why don't you have a lie down on one of the beds upstairs and when you feel better in an hour or so, I'll get you a taxi home.'

A sleep on a nice comfy bed did sound good. That sounded exactly what she needed right then.

She nodded. 'OK.'

With his arm round her shoulders, he guided her upstairs, which took a lot longer than it should because she was so unsteady on her feet. Eventually he guided her inside one of the bedrooms and she sat down on the bed and he sat down next to her, with his arm round her shoulders.

'Can I have a kiss?'

'No,' Orla said, grumpily, knowing she sounded like a petulant child. He was being sweet and trying to help her.

'Well lie back and go to sleep and I'll come and check on you in an hour.'

She lay back on the bed and closed her eyes and as soon as her head touched the pillow, she felt sleep taking her. This was what she needed.

She heard the bedroom door click closed as Kirk left her alone and she snuggled down more into the comfy bed.

She felt a weight on the bed as if someone had sat or knelt on it, which was weird as Kirk had gone but she was too drunk and too tired to open her eyes and after a few moments she thought she'd probably imagined it and the bed was just moving under her own weight. Or maybe the room was just spinning with her stupid drunkenness.

A few seconds later, just as she was dropping off, she felt something touch her stomach and she opened her eyes blearily to find Kirk leaning over her busily trying to undo all the buttons on her shirt dress. He was down to the last two and the rest of her dress lay open.

'What the hell are you doing?' Orla said, grabbing her dress and wrapping it tight around herself.

'Oh, don't be like that, you're going to enjoy it.'

It was like she'd been doused with a bucket of cold water as the harsh reality of what was happening hit her. He'd deliberately got her drunk, he'd brought her up here for this.

She kicked him in the face which sent him sprawling on the bed just as someone tried the clearly locked bedroom door.

'Orla!' Shay's voice came from outside.

'Shay, help!'

A second later the door smashed open and Shay burst into the room. He took in her state of undress, Kirk lying on the bed holding his face and she'd never seen rage like it. Within seconds, he had Kirk pinned up against the wardrobe door by his throat.

'What the hell did you do?' Shay said.

'Nothing I swear,' Kirk said, fear and tears in his eyes.

Orla tried to do her buttons back up, but her hands were shaking too much to work. She looked up just as Shay raised his fist to punch Kirk in the face. Kirk burst into tears which stopped Shay in his tracks.

'Shay, please, I just want to go home,' Orla said, tears choking her own throat.

Shay threw Kirk to the floor and came back to the bed. 'Did he hurt you?'

'No. He just undressed me while I was asleep.'

Shay let out a growl and turned back for Kirk, but she put a hand on his arm, stopping him before he did something he couldn't take back. 'Please, will you take me home?'

He nodded. He moved closer and did her buttons back up, then he wrapped her in a blanket, scooped her up in his arms and carried her out.

The party was still going strong downstairs and no one batted an eyelid as Shay carried her out of the party.

He took her to his car and sat her in the passenger seat, wrapping the blanket tightly around her.

He closed the door and got in the driver's side. 'I haven't been drinking tonight, because I knew I was going to take you home.'

She nodded and he started the car and drove off.

'I'm so sorry,' Orla said.

'What the hell do you have to be sorry for?'

'I saw you and Melody in the summer house, I came to get you as I was feeling unwell, and I saw you kissing and Melody taking her top off. I didn't see any more than that. I'm sorry for ruining your night.'

'You didn't ruin my night. I always planned to take you home and if I wasn't OK with that I wouldn't have offered. And I didn't sleep with Melody because I knew what she was playing at, she was trying to distract me from you. The only one that ruined my night was that little shit

Kirk, how dare he treat you like that. I'm so angry right now.'

'And I'm sorry for making you angry.'

He pulled over sharply onto the side of the road and turned off the engine. 'This is not your fault, do you understand. You didn't do anything wrong.'

Tears fell down her cheeks. He leaned over, unclipped her seatbelt and then hauled her over onto his lap, wrapping his arms tightly around her and she cried against his chest.

'I feel so stupid, I took all these drinks off him believing they were just orange juice and even when I said they tasted funny, he said it was orange and passionfruit and I bloody believed him. How naïve is that? And he was laughing about it with his friends and I didn't realise at the time but he was laughing that he'd got me drunk. And then he said I should go upstairs and lie down for a bit and he'd call me a taxi and I went upstairs with him with no idea what he had planned. I'm such an idiot.'

'It's not your fault. Every woman should be able to go out for drinks and enjoy themselves without worrying that some arsehole is going to take advantage of that. And I'm so sorry I wasn't there, that I allowed myself to get distracted for a few minutes. I saw you in the garden, walking back into the house and I stopped Melody from undressing and told her I had to take you home and then we had a stupid row over it. I would have been there sooner, but I went back in and I was asking everyone where you were, until someone said they'd seen you go upstairs with Kirk and I knew, I knew what he was going to do. I'm so sorry.'

She looked up at him. 'It's not your fault either. Thank you for being there. I'm not sure what would have happened if you hadn't.'

'From where I was standing when I came in, it looked like you were handling it just fine.'

'I kicked him in the face,' Orla said.

'Good, I hope he has a black eye to show for it. I just wish I'd got there sooner.'

'It really wasn't your fault. This is all Kirk. And maybe a tiny bit Melody.'

He smirked.

She kissed him on the cheek and put her head back down on his chest. He stroked his hands up and down her back soothingly.

'I love you, you know,' Orla said.

He kissed the top of her head. 'I love you too.'

She smiled slightly and closed her eyes, breathing him in. He was her harbour in the storm. She was safe when she was with him.

'You're the first person I've said that to. I've not even said that to Mum, Theo or Fern, but of course I love them too,' Shay said.

She looked back up at him. 'Maybe you should tell them.'

He nodded. 'Maybe I should. Shall I take you home?'

'Take me to yours. I don't want my mum to see me like this. She'll call the police.'

'Maybe she should. It would be good to see that arse-hole arrested.'

'He didn't do anything apart from undress me, I can't see that standing up in a court of law.'

'I bet you could still press charges for something,' Shay muttered.

'I'm going to make him pay for this,' Orla said. 'I'll make sure every girl at school and sixth form knows what he did so they know to stay well clear of him. His reputation will be in tatters. That's the very least I can do.'

She clambered off his lap and got back into her seat. Shay drove the short distance to his house and got out. He came round to her side as she was getting out and took her hand and led her into his house. The house was all in darkness with Carrie and Fern away. Judging from the soft snores she could hear as they passed Theo's room, he was fast asleep too. They walked past Shay's room and she stopped him.

'Can I stay with you tonight?'

He blinked in surprise and then nodded. 'Of course. Let me get some pyjamas from Fern's room.'

He disappeared inside his sister's room and came out with a pair. 'These are old, she won't care if you wear these.'

'I'll, umm, get changed in the bathroom.'

He nodded and went into his bedroom. She quickly got changed and then went back to his bedroom. He was already lying in bed, topless, waiting for her. Her heart fluttered nervously, not because she was scared but because it was Shay, the man she'd been in love with for over two years. She climbed into bed next to him and snuggled into his chest. He immediately wrapped his arms around her holding her tight. She closed her eyes and as he stroked her, she felt herself drifting off to sleep. And just as she was right on the edge of sleep, she heard him whisper, 'I love you' again, as if trying those words on for size.

CHAPTER TEN

Present day.

'Orla, wake up, I can't lose you, please wake up.'

CHAPTER ELEVEN

Orla, aged 18. December 5th

Orla climbed down the last few steps to Cranberry Cove and spotted Shay sitting at the back in their usual spot. Despite their Christmas tree twinkling happily behind him, she was too annoyed to be swept up in Christmas joy. She marched over to him.

'Did you punch Ryan Kingsley in the face?'

'Yes I did.'

'Why?'

'He was laughing at you for refusing to have sex with him, called you some not so pleasant names so I punched him.'

Orla sighed and sat next to him. She took his hand and ran her fingers over the sore looking knuckles. 'I don't need you to fight for me. I kicked his ass to the kerb several days ago when he got really arsey with me about sex, or rather the lack of it. He can say what he wants, I don't care.'

Except she did. She hated that everyone knew her business and had their own opinions on it. She hated that the last two guys she'd dated and not had sex with had then gone on to tell all their friends. She felt like she was the town virgin and she would be paraded through the streets wearing a funny hat so everyone could laugh at her.

'What's going on, Orla? Who you do or don't have sex with is none of my business and personally I think you can do a lot better than Ryan Kingsley, but he said you got all freaked out when he started undressing you and he was laughing about it, so I punched him for that too.'

'How many times did you hit him?'

'Maybe three or four.'

She sighed. 'I just... can't do it.'

His hand was still in hers and he slotted his fingers through hers. 'Because of Kirk?'

She nodded. 'It's so silly, it's been two years. After it happened, I was a bit shook up about it for a few days but I told myself I'd handled it, that I kicked him and I'd got the upper hand, despite being drunk. I didn't feel like a victim I felt like... a warrior. And then I got revenge on him by telling everyone what he did, and it felt so good. Like I had won. But then whenever a man would ask me out after that I always said no, I didn't want a relationship with anyone. I just didn't trust anyone enough not to be a complete ass. I think Kirk laughing about it with all his friends at the party really bothered me. Laughing that he'd got me drunk and he was going to take me upstairs and show me a good time and they were all laughing and cheering him on. That's disgusting, isn't it?'

'Yes, it is.'

'And I think the thought of being with a man and him telling all his mates after just really put me off, so I kept saying no. And then I realised that I was being silly – not all men are arseholes. Look at you.'

'Oh yes, I'm the patron saint of decent and virtuous behaviour,' Shay said, dryly.

'Oh shush. You've slept with lots of women and I never hear you bragging about it. I never hear you telling me or any of your other friends how good or bad they were in bed.'

'No, I've never done that.'

'See. Not an arsehole. So I thought there have to be other good men out there too, so I started dating, but every time they brought up sex I bailed, even before it got that far. My girlfriends kept saying that sex isn't a big deal and I just needed to get it over with. So I dated Ben and he seemed nice but when we eventually got around to sex and we were in his room and he started undressing me, I just had this flashback to Kirk, leaning over me, undoing my buttons and it just freaked me out. I didn't want Ben's hands on me, touching me, just like I didn't want Kirk to touch me. I told Ben to stop and got out of there as fast as I could. And then he told all his friends what had happened. Same thing happened with Ryan, but at least Ben didn't get angry with me like Ryan did.'

'Any man who gets angry with you for refusing to have sex is not someone you should be with. You deserve so much better than that.'

'I just feel like I've made it into a much bigger deal than it needs to be, I just want to get it out the way so I can move on with my life and not have Kirk's bad memory have a hold over me. I go to London to start my nine-month chef's apprenticeship in just over a week and then university in September next year. I don't want to be the only virgin at university and I don't want the same thing to happen when I'm there and everyone to laugh at me because I backed out again.'

'You just need to find someone you trust, someone you can explain your concerns to and who's kind enough to go slowly and patiently enough to stop if you get freaked out and try again another time.'

She swallowed. She'd practised this conversation in a hundred different ways but every time she got to this bit, she always cringed with embarrassment.

'I trust you.'

He stared at her, clearly not comprehending for a few seconds before his eyes widened in shock.

'Oh hell no. Orla, I'm not sleeping with you.'

It wasn't the reaction she was hoping for, but then what was she expecting? For him to take her in his arms and make love to her here on the beach under the stars? They'd never had that kind of relationship, there'd never been anything romantic between them.

'Why not, you have lots of meaningless sex with lots of different women. How is this different?'

'Because you're my best friend and I'm not doing that to you.'

'It's just sex, it's no big deal. It would all be over in a few minutes and I can finally move on with my life and not let Kirk ruin it. We can do it here and—'

'No,' he stood up. 'Absolutely not.'

With that he stormed off the beach leaving her alone in the dark.

There was a knocking on her door later that night.

After her dad had finally moved out the year before, her mum had immediately got herself a boyfriend and spent most nights and weekends at his house rather than at home, which was fine with Orla, she liked being alone.

She'd already gone to bed and turned off all the lights, but she knew who it would be. She lay in bed not sure if she wanted to face him or at least not tonight. She was so embarrassed she'd asked Shay to sleep with her. She wasn't really surprised he said no. He knocked again and she got up and pulled on a robe and padded downstairs. Sure enough, his huge frame filled the door outside.

She opened the door and he looked at her.

'Hey, are you OK?' he asked.

'I'm fine. Embarrassed but fine.'

He sighed. 'You shouldn't be embarrassed and I'm sorry for reacting the way I did.'

'You don't need to be sorry. I don't want you to do something you don't want to do.'

'I'm going to do it,' he blurted out.

She looked at him in confusion. 'What?'

'I want to do it.'

'No, you made it very clear you don't.'

'No I do. When I said no when you first asked, it wasn't because I didn't want to, I said no because you deserve someone so much better than me.'

'What? Why would you think that?'

'It's the truth, I don't know why you'd want someone like me to even touch you let alone make love to you, I feel like you're scraping the bottom of the barrel by asking me, but equally out of all the boys in Apple Hill Bay you could choose, I don't know a single one that would treat you with the respect and care that you deserve, so I suppose it has to be me. The boys I go to college with, my friends from school, they'd all be bragging about being your first, you'd probably have a quick fumble in the park or in the back of their car which you wouldn't particularly enjoy and most of them never use protection. I would take care of you.'

'I didn't want a boy, I wanted a man, someone respectful and kind, someone who would make me feel safe in every way. And I'm not scraping the barrel, not at all, I've chosen the very best man I know. And everything you've just said proves that. And I'm so relieved that you're not horrified at the thought of sleeping with me.'

'Far from it, I've thought of nothing else since you suggested it.'

Her heart leapt. 'Really?' That didn't make sense. He'd never looked at her in that way.

'Of course. And I'm sorry if I made you think otherwise.'

She swallowed, nerves suddenly rushing through her. 'So... did you want to come in? Mum's at her boyfriend's for the weekend, so we're alone.'

He shook his head. 'I want to make sure we do this properly and that you will never look back at your first time with regret.'

'I could never regret being with you.'

'If we're doing this, we're doing it my way. It's not going to be some quick meaningless shag. I've rented Starlight Cottage for three nights, Friday 'til Monday on the weekend before you go to London.'

'Shay, no, that's too much. That place costs a fortune, I don't need that, and I don't need three nights.'

'I want it to be special for you.'

She stared at him. God, she loved this man so much.

'But what will we do for three nights?'

'We can chill out, use the pool, watch movies. But I just wanted you to have the time to relax and be ready. We can take our time and if you get scared, we can stop and try again later. And if you don't like it, we can try different positions to see if that helps.'

'Different positions,' Orla squeaked. One of her favourite magazines had a page in every issue called Position of the Fortnight, which detailed various different sexual positions and how to do them. She'd always looked at them in the same way you might view a contortionist, none of them looked viable or even that comfortable. The idea of Shay doing some of those with her was more than a little intimidating.

He smiled slightly. 'Some positions are a lot more pleasurable for the woman than others. We can try a few to see what you like.'

'A few? Did you plan to spend the whole weekend having sex?'

He stared at her. 'If that's what you want.'

She had no words at all. She imagined it would be a few minutes and it would be over. Now he was talking about having a full weekend of sex with a variety of positions. Why did she suddenly feel like a fish out of water?

'You don't need to worry, we'll only do what you're comfortable with.'

'OK,' she said, quietly.

'I should go. I'm going on this training course tomorrow for the week, so I won't see you now till Friday. We can get the keys for Starlight Cottage at three, so I'll pick you up just before.'

She nodded. She watched him walk down towards the gate then he turned back.

'If you're nervous or you have any questions, you can call me while I'm away and we can talk.'

'OK.'

He gave her a little wave and it suddenly felt awkward. They both knew that the next time they'd be seeing each other they'd be having sex. It barely seemed real, not after all this time. But if it was awkward now, what would it be like after they'd done it?

'Shay.' He stopped as he moved away.

She ran out to him, her bare feet getting wet on the dewy grass.

'This isn't going to ruin our friendship, is it? I don't want to lose you.'

He shook his head. 'There's nothing that could ruin that. What we have is unbreakable.'

She nodded. He gave her a hug and kissed her on the top of her head and it was weird to think that the next time he kissed her it would be a lot more intimately.

He let her go and walked off down the hill and she went back inside, her heart racing at what next weekend would hold.

She saw one of her magazines lying on the kitchen table, she had some of the older copies upstairs too. Maybe it was time to do some research.

CHAPTER TWELVE

Orla, aged 18. December 11ᵗʰ

Orla paced nervously inside her house as she waited for Shay to come and pick her up. She'd told her mum she was going away with Shay for the weekend and her mum had just waved and told her to have a good time as she ran out the door to be with her boyfriend. But they'd never been close through Orla's teenage years, not since the fighting started between her parents. She'd kind of wanted to talk to her mum about all this but they just didn't have that kind of relationship. The only person she'd really wanted to talk to about what was happening this weekend was Fern, but somehow sleeping with her friend's brother didn't come up easily in conversation.

Shay pulled up in his car and there was part of her that wanted to run away and hide. She wasn't scared, she trusted Shay, but this whole weekend of sex that was on offer was definitely more than a little bit intimidating.

She opened the door and wheeled her suitcase to the entrance. What did you pack for a weekend of sex with your best friend? She didn't have any sexy underwear and was too embarrassed to go and buy any in case he thought she was trying too hard. It was some weird line they were going to cross. They were going to have sex, but they weren't together, they weren't a couple, so sexy underwear seemed like a step too far.

He came to the door and lifted her suitcase. He laughed. 'Did you pack anything? This is very light.'

'Just a few clothes. A couple of bikinis for the pool, which thankfully is indoors, and a jumper. I didn't think I'd need a lot of clothes.'

She felt her cheeks flame at what she'd said. 'I didn't mean...'

'You're right, we'll probably be in the pool quite a bit,' Shay skated over it. 'Are you ready?'

She felt her eyes widen – did he mean ready for sex? Would they be doing it as soon as they walked through the door of the cottage?

'To go?' He quickly clarified.

She nodded and he walked out to the car and put her case in the boot. She watched him. He hadn't given her a kiss on the cheek to say hello but of course he wouldn't, he wasn't her boyfriend. They were just friends and he was behaving exactly as he always had, as if this weekend was nothing more than two friends hanging out. Yet in half an hour they could be having sex for the first time, and it would also be the first time they'd kiss and that just felt a bit backward – surely they should at least kiss first.

She closed the door and followed him out to the car. She got in and he drove off. He put the heating on and soon the car was filled with warmth. It was a freezing cold start to December, there was even talk of snow.

'How was the course?' Orla asked, clinging to the normality.

'It was really good, really practical and we worked with some great experts in their trade,' Shay said, driving the car over the hill so Starlight Cottage came into view. They both fell quiet.

'Are you OK?' Shay asked.

She nodded.

'I have to admit, I've never felt this nervous about sex before,' Shay said.

She laughed in relief. 'You're nervous too?'

'Of course. It's you. This feels way more significant than any woman I've been with before. It feels like it means more. And I know it's not, I know this is just sex for you but it's us, together, and it means something to me.'

Her heart leapt. 'It means something to me too.'

He smiled and took her hand.

She frowned in confusion as she watched him driving along. She was ninety-nine percent sure he didn't have feelings for her, not in that way. But it meant something to her because she was going to be with the man she had been in love with ever since they'd first met. So why did it mean something to him? She supposed their friendship added another layer to it for him, that he'd not experienced in other relationships, he had to mean that. She couldn't start looking for something that wasn't there in all of this.

He pulled up outside Starlight Cottage and her heart was hammering against her chest. They sat staring at it for a few moments, feeling the weight of what was going to happen beyond those doors.

'I am yours for the whole weekend,' Shay said. 'Whatever you do or don't want to do, I'm happy. If you want to try every position in the Kama Sutra in every room in the house, I'm game. If you decide you just want to swim in the pool and hang out and watch movies and not have sex, that's fine too, it'll be a nice way to say goodbye before you go to London for your big patisserie apprenticeship. I also want you to know I have never had sex without a condom but also I've just had a health check to make sure I was clean for you, and I am.'

Her heart swelled with love for him for taking this so seriously. She stroked his face and he blinked in surprise at her touch. They didn't have this intimacy but hell, they were going to be a lot more intimate than that soon enough.

They got out the car and started taking stuff into the house. Shay had packed a lot of food; it appeared he was going to do a lot of cooking for her.

'Let me give you some money towards all this. This is a lot of food.'

'No, absolutely not. This weekend is on me.'

'That doesn't seem fair.'

'It seems more than fair to me,' Shay said, bringing the last of the bags into the house.

Shay started putting some of the cold items in the fridge and freezer and Orla looked around the house. It was modern and clean looking and the view over Cranberry Cove and the rest of Apple Hill Bay was beautiful in the frosty afternoon. There was an indoor pool in the back part of the house, the turquoise of the tiles sparkling under the tiny spotlights, the fold-up doors currently open, letting in some of the weak winter sunshine. It was lovely.

The house had been decorated beautifully for Christmas with a tree sparkling under the weight of a multitude of gold baubles and white lights. There was a gorgeous garland wrapped around the banister and over the mantelpiece of the huge open fireplace and there were cute little Christmas gnomes in various Christmas sweaters positioned all around the house.

'What do you think? Is it OK?' Shay asked.

'It's beautiful,' Orla said.

They stared at each other and she wondered if he would just pick up her up now and carry her upstairs to the bedroom, although it looked like he wasn't going to do that. She decided they might as well make a start. Despite his magnanimous attitude to not having sex this weekend, they were here to do just that. She started undoing the buttons on her shirt and cursed that her fingers were shaking.

He closed his hand over hers. 'What are you doing?'

She looked at him in confusion. 'What we're here to do.'

He frowned. 'I'm not in any rush, we have the whole weekend to do that, we'll get to it when you're ready. If you're ready.'

'I am ready.'

'Really, because you're trembling like a leaf.'

She let out a breath. 'I'm just a bit nervous.'

'OK, let's talk about that so I can help you. What are you nervous about? You said you trusted me.'

'I do, it's just...'

'Are you afraid it will hurt.'

'No, I umm... I have toys.' She felt her cheeks flush.

'Toys?'

'Do you want me to spell it out to you.'

He cleared his throat. 'No, I've got the picture.'

'Well, it's never hurt when I've umm... you know. So I don't think it will hurt with you, but then I imagine you're significantly bigger than some of my umm... toys so maybe it will.'

'I'm going to go really slow, so I really hope it won't, but if you're not nervous about that then what are you nervous about?'

'Well by all accounts, you're very experienced in these matters and I'm not at all and, I know you didn't even want to do it with me and I don't blame you because you're probably not going to enjoy it. But—'

'Orla this weekend is about you not about me, but you can rest assured that I absolutely will enjoy it.'

She stared at him, her mouth dry.

'I think I'll go for a swim in the pool. I need to cool off. Why don't you join me?' Shay said.

He grabbed both their bags and ran upstairs and after a few moments he appeared, just wearing his swim shorts. His chest was a glorious thing, all muscly and tanned from his days working out in the sun. His legs were strong and muscly too. He walked into the pool room and dived into the pool.

She went upstairs and changed into her bikini and went back downstairs again. She loved the way he looked at her as she walked into the room with the pool. It made her feel powerful. She dived in, swam underwater the length of the pool and surfaced next to him. She enjoyed the way the water droplets on his skin glistened under the spotlights.

'You know, it'll be weird if we sleep together later and we've never even kissed,' Orla said.

He frowned and she wondered if she'd pushed it too far.

'You want me to kiss you?'

'I presume we will probably kiss a bit when we...'

'Make love,' Shay said.

'Yeah.'

'I'd planned on kissing you all over.'

She stared at him. He was going to ruin her. How was she ever going to survive this weekend with her heart intact when he was looking at her like that and saying these things? She had to keep reminding herself it was just sex.

'I like the sound of that. But don't you think it'd be

weird if the first time your mouth touches me, it's on my breast not my mouth.'

He smirked. 'When you put it like that, yes. Would you like me to kiss you?'

She nodded.

He stroked her face, tracing his thumb over her lips. She was thrown by the look of emotion on his face, it was one of complete adoration. He bent his head and kissed her. Her heart thundered in her chest. She'd dreamt of this moment for years and never thought it would happen. And yes, it was happening under very weird circumstances, but for one moment she was going to pretend it was all real. His kiss was so gentle to start with, the taste of him was magnificent. She slid her arms round his neck, pressing herself up against him and relishing in the feel of his wet, hard chest against hers. This kiss was the sexiest, hottest kiss of her life. Admittedly, she'd only kissed a few boys, but this was something different, there was so much passion and heat in this kiss.

Feeling bold, she ran her hand down the muscles in his arm and then over his chest and he made a strangled noise against her mouth. He moved his hands down to her hips, his thumbs tracing the side straps of her bikini, it made her stomach clench with desire. He wrapped his arms around her holding her close so she could feel every hard edge of him against her and she had never felt so safe in her whole life.

And then she felt something else, how much he wanted her. He was rock hard. She gasped in shock against his lips and pulled back to look at him, she couldn't believe he was so turned on from a simple kiss.

'Sorry, just ignore it,' he muttered. He went to kiss her again, but she stopped him.

'What if I don't want to ignore it.'

She ran her hands down his chest towards the waistband of his shorts. All fears, worries and doubts vanished in an instant. He wanted her as much as she wanted him and that made her feel like a goddess. He caught her hand with a groan.

'Orla, I wanted you to have time to relax before we did anything, I didn't want to pounce on you as soon as you walked through the door.'

'What if I want you to pounce on me?'

'I'm trying really hard to be respectful here, but you don't know what you do to me.'

'Then show me.'

He swallowed. 'Can I touch you?'

She nodded and he moved his hands to her chest, stroking across her shoulders and just under her neck and she felt bad that she had never asked him before she ran her hands over his chest.

'Can I touch you?'

He chuckled. 'You can do whatever you want with me, I'm yours for the weekend, remember.'

She smoothed her hands across his chest, tracing every hard edge of his muscles and his abs. He really was so beautiful. Her breath caught in her throat when he traced his fingers over the edge of her bikini top towards her heart, touching her breasts with barely a whisper but it was enough to make her ache in ways she had never felt before. How could he affect her with such a simple, gentle touch?

He slowly undid the little straps at the side of the bikini top and slid the straps down her arms then threw the top onto the side of the pool and she watched his eyes darken with need. She looked out into the garden, but they were completely secluded there. There were no other houses on this side of the bay and while the other side of the house opened out onto the spectacular view of the bay, this area was completely closed off from view. An eight-foot brick wall surrounded the small garden area here and there were trees and bushes growing along the top. No one would see them here.

'Promise me something,' he said, his voice rough. 'If I do something you don't like or if it moves too fast for you, or you change your mind, you'll tell me.'

She nodded, her mouth dry.

'Promise me.'

'I promise.'

He stroked his hands across her breasts, making her breath hitch. He leaned forward and kissed her throat just under her ear, making goosebumps erupt across her skin, as his hands continued to caress her breasts, her stomach, her back. Every touch was making her more needy and desperate for him. He trailed his mouth lower, capturing her breast in the sweetest, hottest kiss that made her cry out.

He lifted his head, 'OK?'

She nodded. 'Definitely OK.'

He smiled and kissed her hard. He lifted her and she wrapped her legs around his hips as he walked up the steps carrying her out of the pool. He lay her down on a large sun lounger and she felt relieved and excited this was finally going to happen. He lay down next to her, still kissing her, and he made quick work of undoing the straps on her bikini bottoms and tossing it to one side. She reached for his shorts, but he caught her hand.

'Not yet.'

She let out a moan of frustration and he chuckled. 'It's OK, I'm going to take care of you. Tell me, when you use your toys, what is it you think about?'

She felt her cheeks flush because she always thought of him, imagined it was him touching her. 'I can't tell you that.'

'Why not?'

'Because you'll laugh.'

'I promise I won't.'

She shook her head.

'OK, show me how you touch yourself.'

'I'm not doing that either, that's too embarrassing having you watch that.'

'It's nothing to be embarrassed about.'

She shook her head again.

'OK, take my hand and use it to touch yourself, close your eyes, picture your deepest fantasy and work your magic.'

She hesitated for a moment then took his hand. She didn't close her eyes because she wanted to remember this vividly, but she took his hand and guided it between her legs to the spot she needed him most.

'There,' she whispered.

He moved his fingers a few times and she arched off the bed with a cry.

'Like that?' he asked.

'Yes,' she bit out.

The difference between her fantasies and reality were miles apart – his touch was strong and confident but gentle and loving at the same time. She took her hand away, letting him take over and it was utterly divine, it was everything she needed and more. His eyes were on hers the whole time as he brought her hurtling over the edge, screaming and crying out all kinds of noises she'd never made before.

As she came down from her high, her breath ragged, he got to his feet and scooped her up in his arms.

'What are you doing?'

'We need to take this upstairs. You carry on screaming like that, people are going to be calling the police thinking I'm murdering you.'

She laughed as she wrapped her arms round his neck. 'I wasn't that loud.'

'You were, but I intend to make you scream louder, I want to hear you screaming out my name.'

He carried her upstairs and lay her down on the bed, lying on top of her and kissing her. He pulled back slightly to look at her, stroking her hair. 'You still doing OK?'

'Yes.'

'We can stop if you want?'

'Don't stop.'

He kissed her again and then kissed her throat, her chest, trailing his hot mouth lower across her stomach and then he kissed her right there between her legs, making her cry out again.

'Shay.' She ran her hand through his hair, fisting her other hand in the sheet as he made her feel things she'd never felt before. She'd barely had chance to draw breath before her orgasm slammed into her so hard that for a second, she thought she was seeing stars. She shouted out his name, writhing on the bed, but he didn't stop, wringing out every last drop of pleasure from her until she was breathing so hard it was like she'd run a marathon.

Finally, he stopped and knelt up between her legs. 'You still OK?'

She nodded, too exhausted to speak.

'You want me to carry on?'

'Yes, I need you.'

'Let me just grab a condom from my bag.'

She reached out to stop him. 'I'm on the pill so you don't need to, if you don't want to.'

He stared at her.

'You're clean, I'm clean, but it's your call. I totally understand if you'd prefer to use one.' Orla said.

'No, I want to feel you.' he said, his voice was rough. He leaned over her, shifting her legs further apart to accommodate his large frame.

'You let me know if it hurts.'

She stroked his face. 'I trust you.'

'Keep your eyes on mine, I want to see if you're OK.'

She smiled up at him, his face filled with so much concern and then she felt him pushing slowly inside her. She suppressed the gasp of surprise at how big he felt inside her, but she didn't want to worry him and it didn't hurt, she felt so deliciously full of him.

He eased himself carefully out and moved back inside, so slowly and gently.

'Are you OK?' Shay asked.

'Yes.' She could see every muscle in his body was tensed. 'Are you? You look tense, are you not enjoying it?'

'Orla being with you is like winning the lottery but I'm trying really hard not to hurt you.'

'I'm OK, I promise, you can relax, I'm not made of china.'

He let out a breath he'd clearly been holding. 'You sure?'

'Don't hold yourself back for me.'

He settled himself between her legs and she wrapped her arms and legs around him, taking him deeper. He started moving faster but every move was still careful and gentle and it made her fall in love with him so much more. He was right, no other man would have taken this much care of her. He felt so divine, every touch, every movement from him was pure bliss, pleasure radiating through her. She started moving with him, her body responding to his almost instinctively.

'You feel so good,' Shay said, breathlessly.

The noise she made in response sounded like an animal in pain, which caused him to stop for a second.

'You OK?'

She laughed, 'Yes sorry, I'm not sure what that was, don't stop.'

He smiled and started moving against her again and that pleasure started building until it felt like every nerve was on fire, she stroked his face and the look of complete love on his face made her heart soar and sent her hurtling over the edge, taking him with her, shouting out his name, making all manner of noises.

He stared down at her in complete awe, his breath heavy against her lips, then he rolled off her, bringing her with him so she was lying half on top of him and while she was still trying to catch her breath, he kissed her hard.

Orla couldn't believe that had just happened. Whenever her friends talked about sex, they always said how they never really enjoyed it, that years of reading romance novels had set them up for a big disappointment, but making love with Shay had been glorious, not only because he had taken so much care with her, or even because being with him had been every fantasy come true, but it had been utterly incredible too and she just hadn't been expecting that.

He was stroking her back as she lay on his chest and she looked up at him.

He watched her, his eyes filled with concern. 'Was it OK?'

She smiled. 'It was definitely more than OK, it was magnificent.' She paused. 'Was it... was it OK for you?'

He grinned. 'Best sex I've ever had.'

She laughed. 'That's very nice of you to say but—'

'It's true. I'm not sure whether it was so good because it's you and I... You mean the world to me, and most of the women I've been with I haven't felt anything for, I never cared about them the way I care about you, but hands down it was the best sex of my life.'

Her heart leapt at this. She knew part of the reason why it had been so wonderful for her had been because she loved him. She suddenly wondered if he felt the same too.

She shook her head before she let herself go down that path. 'Well thank you.'

'You don't need to thank me, I enjoyed it immensely.'

'No thank you for just being so sweet and kind and considerate, and thank you for all this,' she gestured to the house.

'Oh, of course.'

She chewed her lip. It suddenly felt awkward between them and she didn't want that. Had they crossed that boundary and now they could never go back?

'So... what happens now?'

He cleared his throat. 'That's entirely up to you. I can take you home right now or we can hang out in this lovely house all weekend, using the pool, watch TV together or...' he trailed off.

'Or?'

'Or we can spend the rest of the weekend having sex in

every room of the house starting with having a shower together.'

She grinned and stroked a hand across his chest. 'A whole weekend of sex sounds perfect to me.'

He smiled in relief and kissed her then stood up and scooped her up in his arms, which made her giggle, and carried her off to the shower.

CHAPTER THIRTEEN

Orla, aged 18. December 14th

It had been a glorious weekend with Shay. He had been true to his word and made love to her in every room of the house, but even when they hadn't been doing that he had cuddled and kissed her as if he simply couldn't get enough of her. When they were having sex, he would look at her as if he was completely in love with her and impossibly, she knew she had fallen even more in love with him.

And she'd decided to tell him.

She couldn't believe that after that incredible weekend of kissing, cuddling and making love he didn't feel the same way. Maybe he'd felt this way for years, just like she had, but neither of them had been brave enough to tell each other. Maybe they needed this weekend to make everything come to a head. She was going to London for her apprenticeship tomorrow, but they could make it work. She could come back here on holidays and weekends. He could come and visit her.

'We should go,' Shay said in between his kisses. They were due to check out of the house in the next half-hour and they were all packed ready to go but Shay had been keen to make the most of the cottage and made love to her one more time. Now they were lying in bed, kissing.

'Shay.'

'Mmm?' Shay said, still enjoying the kissing.

She giggled against his mouth, and he pulled back to look at her, affection for her in his eyes. She stroked his face. 'I love you.'

For a brief second, she thought he was going to say it back, that he was going to kiss her and tell her he'd always been in love with her too. His eyes lit up and there was a smile on his face before his face changed. His eyes widened in horror. 'No, Orla, you can't love me.'

He quickly got out of bed and started throwing clothes on.

'But I do.'

'No. This was just sex. Great sex admittedly, but it didn't mean anything. You're getting confused between wonderful sex and the emotions that can develop because of that and a deeper connection of love. This isn't love.'

'I'm not confused, Shay. I've been in love with you for years. I know how I feel.'

He threw her clothes on the bed. 'Get dressed, we need to go.'

With that he stormed out the room.

What the hell had just happened? How could her beautiful, perfect weekend have suddenly ended so badly? How could he not feel the same? She'd seen it in his eyes, felt it in his touch. He had spent the whole weekend touching her in some way, he had stroked her, cuddled her, or even held her hand as they watched TV as if he didn't want to be apart from her. Sometimes, he would just lie in bed or on the sofa stroking her and kissing her, even if they weren't making love. Why would he do that if it was just sex? Nothing about this weekend had been meaningless. It had been beautiful because he had been so affectionate and loving towards her. He loved her, she knew that in every fibre of her soul.

She got out of bed and quickly threw her clothes on and ran downstairs to see him throwing their bags into the boot of his car.

'Shay.'

He didn't even look up from loading the boot.

'God damn it Shay, at least have the courtesy to look at me.'

He sighed, closed the boot and came back to her as she stood in the doorway.

'I love you, with everything I have. And I know you love me too, I know you do.'

He shook his head and looked away. 'You need to aim higher Orla. You're going to your big apprenticeship in London and then on to university. You're going to make something of your life, be somebody, not some nobody with zero prospects. You're going to be some amazing chef someday, cooking for the rich and famous in your own restaurant in some swanky city. Have higher standards for yourself.'

'I have the very highest standards. Which is why I'm in love with the kindest, most amazing, brilliant man I've ever met.'

'I'm none of those things.'

'Is this just your self-doubt and self-hate kicking in. You think you don't deserve to be loved. You couldn't be more wrong. Do you think any other man would have treated me with so much care and respect this weekend? Would any other man have gone to this much trouble, renting a cottage just to make sure that my first time was special? Would any other man give up a night of sex with his girlfriend just to make sure I get home safely from a party? You are the kindest, most generous, decent man I've ever met. You deserve to be loved, you are loved, and I won't let you discredit, dismiss or patronise my feelings for you. I love you.'

'You're being ridiculous.' He walked into the house and came back a few moments later, closing the door behind him. He locked the door and popped the key into the key safe. 'Let's get you home.'

'No.' Orla said, folding her arms across her chest.

'What?'

'For once in your life, be bold, be courageous, take a risk and tell me you love me too. I know I'm going to London, but we can make it work somehow. I can come back at weekends and during the holidays. You can come and visit me in London. Just tell me you love me and we can figure it out.'

Shay looked away and shook his head.

'Or tell me you don't love me. Look me in the eye and tell me you don't love me and I'll walk away now. I'll go to London, and we can forget this whole weekend ever happened.'

He didn't speak for the longest time and that didn't bode well. Surely if you loved someone and they loved you, you'd shout your feelings for them from the rooftops.

He turned back to her. 'I don't love you Orla. I'm sorry, I don't feel that way. It was just sex.'

She felt her heart shatter. How could she have got this so wrong?

She nodded and got in the car, willing herself not to cry. He got in the car too and they drove back to hers in complete silence. Tears fell down her cheeks as she stared out the window and she quickly wiped them away, not wanting him to see.

He pulled up outside her house and she was desperate to get away from him. She was so embarrassed, so hurt, she just wanted to curl up on her bed and sob.

'Thanks for a lovely weekend,' Orla said, not looking at him.

'I umm… I guess I'll see you when you come back for Christmas in a few weeks.'

There was no way she could face that. She shook her head. 'No you won't. My mum is talking about going to Scotland with her new boyfriend for Christmas. Dad has already moved to Newquay with his girlfriend. In fact, I'm never coming back here. I have nothing to come back for, not anymore.'

'You have Fern.'

'I'll always stay in touch with her.'

'And… we can still be friends.'

She shook her head. 'I never knew what it felt like when people talked about being broken-hearted until today. There isn't any coming back from this.' She swallowed a sob that threatened to escape but more tears fell from her eyes. She quickly wiped them away. 'I can't come back here and watch you go off with random women you don't even like. I can't come back here and see you or talk to you without remembering this… pain I'm feeling or without remembering this beautiful weekend and how it meant nothing to you. This has to be the end. Goodbye Shay.'

She got out the car, hurried round to the boot, grabbed her bag and ran up the garden path.

'Orla, wait.' Shay was out of the car, but she quickly opened the front door and closed and locked it as soon as she got inside. She ran upstairs as she heard him hammering on the door. She threw herself down on her bed and burst into tears.

CHAPTER FOURTEEN

Present day

Shay carefully scooped Orla up into his arms and stumbled along the beach towards the stairs that would lead to Starlight Cottage. She was icy cold and completely unresponsive. Fear flooded through him. He couldn't lose her. But what if he was doing more damage than good moving her around?

He lay her down gently on the sand again and looked around. Their Christmas tree twinkled at the back of the beach in the opening to a cave, almost taunting him of happier times and all those years that he'd never told her how he truly felt.

He looked back at her and stroked her face. 'Come on baby, wake up, please, I love you.'

CHAPTER FIFTEEN

Orla, aged 24. December 15th

What was she doing here? It had been six years since she'd set foot in Apple Hill Bay, swearing she'd never return, and yet here she was.

She'd spent nine months doing an apprenticeship in one of the best hotels in London and then three years at university, learning the hospitality trade and everything she needed to know about becoming a chef and running a restaurant, before two and a half years working at various different levels in cafés and restaurants in London, mostly working as a pastry chef but doing other types of cooking too. But it had always been her dream to have her own place one day. Nothing grand, but hers.

She'd stayed in contact with Fern over the years and surprisingly, with Carrie too, and when Carrie had offered her the opportunity to run Seahorses, the café she was opening as part of her new Beach Hut Hotel, she had leapt at the chance. Well, she had deliberated over it for several days before accepting, writing a list of all the pros and cons. Pros being she would have her own café, make all the decisions, be in charge of the running of the place, she could make her own cakes and desserts, she'd get invaluable experience, she would be back in Apple Hill Bay, a beautiful place she had loved for many years, and she'd get to see more of Fern and Carrie. In fact, the list of reasons why she should grab the chance with both hands had filled a page. The list of cons was just one. Shay.

She hadn't seen or spoken to him since that glorious weekend and that heartbreaking end to their friendship. He had called, texted, emailed, and she had ignored every single one. He'd even wanted to come down to London to see her but when Fern asked if she could give him the address, Orla had said no and Fern never knew why.

Eventually he'd given up. For months afterwards, Orla had cried in her room at night, not only because he didn't love her, but for the loss of their friendship too. Looking back, Orla knew she had acted like a child, cutting him out of her life, especially when he had pulled out all the stops to give her such a beautiful weekend. But she had been young, and everything had been so black and white back then. He didn't love her so she couldn't see him anymore. She regretted that more than anything. She'd been heartbroken but she should never have walked away from their friendship.

She'd tried to move on from the heartache; she'd dated

lots of men, some of them had even lasted a few months, but none of them had filled the massive hole in her heart that Shay had left. She'd loved some of them too, but never with the same intensity that she'd loved Shay. And while the sex had been nice and sometimes good, it had never been as incredible as making love to Shay. She wasn't sure whether that was because she'd been head over heels in love with him, or because he'd taken so much care of her that weekend, making sure her pleasure was the most important thing or because he really was a god of sex, but he had set the bar impossibly high and no one else could compare to him, physically or emotionally.

So the possibility of seeing Shay again had been one big down side. How could she ever get over him if she was seeing him every day? What would it feel like to see him with other women? How awkward would it be to see him for the first time when her behaviour had been so bad at the end?

But then she'd reasoned he would probably want to avoid her too and how often would she realistically see him? And if she did see him, she was a grown-ass woman now, she could act sensibly and maturely. Make polite conversation.

So she'd said yes to Carrie and after a few weeks of discussing what Orla wanted for the café, and a few weeks' notice in her old job, she had moved back to Apple Hill Bay two days before they were due to open. She'd rented a little flat that came fully furnished, so she just moved straight in with her stuff.

The café looked beautifully decorated for Christmas,

with trees and festive table arrangements and Orla had been busy making gingerbread men, decorated Christmas cookies, mince pies and Christmas pudding flavoured fudge ready to sell to the customers.

She was excited. Mostly.

She'd told herself again and again that it would probably be weeks before she bumped into Shay, especially with the two of them avoiding each other like the plague, but it seemed like someone had forgot to tell Shay, as ten minutes before Seahorses was due to open for the first time, he was walking towards it with a bunch of flowers in his hand.

Oh God, what was she going to say to him? She hadn't had time to prepare anything, she didn't think she'd be seeing him again so soon. All those feelings she had tried to bury over the last six years came flooding back, all that pain she felt when he said he didn't love her, the humiliation of insisting he did love her when he didn't. And she *still* loved him, that had never gone away, no matter how hard she tried. She owed him an apology, but she didn't know where to even begin with that.

He had grown to be so big and broad – this was not the boy she left behind. He was definitely all man and it just made those feelings she had for him so much more intense. He drew closer and all she could remember was his glorious body pinning her to the bed, his mouth kissing every single part of her, the way he stroked and caressed her with such adoration, the way he had made her scream out his name so many times over that weekend she'd lost count.

'Who's the hottie?' Ettie, her assistant said as she came out the kitchen. She wasn't from Apple Hill Bay so didn't know any of the locals – hell, Orla didn't know half of them anymore.

'A friend, an old friend,' Orla quickly clarified. 'I haven't spoken to him in six years.'

'An ex?'

'No.'

'So, why are you looking at him as if you'd like to eat him?'

'I wasn't.'

'Sure you weren't. I'll erm... be in the kitchen if you need me.'

Orla wanted to say she definitely needed her, but Shay was already opening the café door and Ettie was gone.

She felt her cheeks flame as she stared at him. She had no idea what she was going to say to him.

He moved over to the counter and his eyes raked over her as if he couldn't get enough of looking at her.

'Hi Orla.'

She cleared her throat, trying to push all those intimate moments she had shared with this man out of her head. 'Hi.'

They stared at each other, the silence dragging on. All the things she wanted to say had fled and all she was left with was an overwhelming desire to lean across the counter and kiss him. But she couldn't humiliate herself like that again.

He offered out the flowers, a gorgeous Christmas

bouquet of poinsettias, holly, berries and white roses. 'I brought you these to say good luck for today.'

She stared at them and then took the flowers. Of all the ways she had envisaged how their first meeting would go, she had not imagined it would include him giving her flowers.

'Thank you, that's really kind and totally unexpected.'

He stared at her looking like he had a hundred things he wanted to say too.

'I umm… I'll be working next door at the Little Beach Hut Hotel, I'm helping to build the next thirty huts and I'm manager of the hotel and the current ten huts, so we'll be seeing each other a lot. I wanted to say hello so it wasn't awkward between us.'

She nodded. It was definitely going to be awkward between them, especially as she'd be seeing him every day.

He opened his mouth to say something else just as the door opened and the local WI group came in, all chatting and laughing between themselves. Carrie had put the word out to local groups and they'd all promised to come and support the new café.

Shay turned round to look at them and she saw his shoulders slump. He turned back. 'I'll let you get on. I'm sure Seahorses will be a brilliant success. It's erm… good to have you back.'

She watched him go, wanting to call him back and say something but she didn't know what. He walked out the door and then suddenly she had a queue in front of her. As she started taking orders. She vowed she would know what to say the next time she saw him.

Orla walked up to the back of Starlight Cottage. The cottage looked like there was someone living there now rather than just tourists staying for a week or so; there were personal photos on the walls and the place looked a lot more lived in. But there was no sign of anyone, so she took the chance and went down the steps to Cranberry Cove.

She was half hoping Shay would be there and half hoping she'd never have the awkwardness of seeing him again, so when she got to the bottom and saw him sitting on the sand, she didn't know whether to be happy or cringe with embarrassment. But she took a deep breath and went over and sat next to him, just like they'd always done.

'I was hoping you'd come here.' Shay said.

'Old habits die hard.'

'How was your first day?' Shay asked.

'Really good, thanks, really busy so that was nice.'

He nodded and they lapsed into silence which wasn't easy or comfortable.

'Look, there's no easy way to say any of this, but I wanted you to know that I had counselling, a lot of it,' Shay said. 'You were right, I was filled with so much self-loathing after my not so auspicious start in life and I never realised how damaging that was to my relationships with people until I lost you. You made me want to be a better man and that started with learning to like myself, so I didn't push people away when they tried to get close.'

She wasn't sure where he was going with this. 'I'm happy for you. I always thought you were an incredible man, I'm glad you can now see that too.'

'And I want you to know how sorry I am,' Shay started.

'What on earth do you have to be sorry about?' Orla said. 'I'm the one who should be sorry.'

He blinked in confusion. 'Why are you sorry?'

'Because I ruined everything. I was the one that asked you to sleep with me when you didn't want to, I'm the one that made it into something it wasn't, that saw something that simply wasn't there, that had never been there, and I'm the one that behaved like a child that had been told they couldn't have a much-longed-for toy and threw a tantrum that drove us apart.'

'Orla, I broke your heart and if I could go back and do that weekend again, it never would have ended that way.'

'I feel that too, I wish I'd never said... what I said. I regret that more than anything. And you didn't break my heart. I was a child. I didn't know what love was. It was just because you gave me such a beautiful, perfect weekend and I didn't want that to end.'

He looked surprised by this. 'But you said you'd loved me for years.'

'As friends, I loved you as a friend and like you said, I was confusing that with the emotions surrounding sex.' She knew that was a lie, but if he thought she didn't really love him maybe they could move past this awkwardness.

'Right.'

They lapsed into another awkward silence.

'I missed you,' Orla said, quietly.

'I missed you too.'

'I don't know if we can ever go back to what we had but—'

'We can go back,' he said, quickly.

'We can?'

'I'd really like to be friends again.'

She looked at him. Was she just setting herself up for a lifetime of torture being here and being friends with him again? But this was the opportunity she wanted, to have him back in her life again. She had messed up spectacularly and he was giving her a get-out-of-jail-free card.

'OK, friends, and we'll just forget that weekend ever happened,' Orla said.

He cleared his throat. 'I'm not sure I can do that, but if that's what it takes to have you back in my life, I promise never to mention it again.'

'Deal.'

CHAPTER SIXTEEN

Present day.

Shay knew he needed to do something, Orla could have serious internal injuries including to her brain and the sooner he got help the better. And even if she had miraculously escaped anything serious, she could get hypothermia unless he got her warm and dry soon.

He very carefully scooped her up and started walking up the stairs towards Starlight Cottage, but every bone in his body was aching. She wasn't heavy but he had never cursed these one hundred and thirteen steps as much as he did now, and he was trying to climb them very slowly so as not to jostle her.

Panic and fear pushed him on. He had to get help, she had to be OK, she just had to be.

He got to the top of the steps and he quickly made his

way to the back door. He lay her down very carefully on one of the sun loungers that was in a covered part of the garden and moved over to the mat by the back door. He cleared it of snow and lifted it, and his heart sank. The spare key wasn't there. He desperately cleared the snow from the ground in the area surrounding the mat just in case it had shifted, but it wasn't there. He must have used it at some point and never put it back.

He stood back up and glanced over at Orla. She was so pale.

He was going to have to break in and though there were many crappy things he had done in his misspent youth, breaking into someone's house hadn't been one of them. He didn't know the first thing about how he could break into his own house. He needed some tools, but they were all locked away in the garage. He could throw a brick through a window but what would that achieve? All the windows were locked so throwing a brick through one wouldn't mean he could reach through the hole and open it from the inside. The backdoor didn't have a handy key positioned in the lock like he saw on many a TV programme. He supposed if he broke enough of the glass, he could crawl through one of the larger windows and find a spare key somewhere inside.

He grabbed a large stone and weighed it up in his hand. He wasn't sure it was big enough to cause any damage and for the first time he was grateful his puppy, Ivy, was deaf and him breaking in wouldn't scare her.

He threw the stone at the window and then ducked as it bounced off the glass leaving it completely unscathed.

He picked it up and tried again to the same result. Any other time this would be funny, but right now he was too scared for Orla to find any humour in this.

He grabbed a brick but instead of throwing it, he wrapped his hand in his jacket and used the brick to smash the window, sending shards of glass everywhere. He cleared all the glass from the pane, which was taking way too long and then he took his jacket off and lay it down over the glass so he could crawl through into the house.

Once he was inside, he ran through to the kitchen, briefly noticing that Ivy was fast asleep on the sofa and that there was toilet paper strewn across the lounge. He knew he really should crate her when he left the house, but it made her so distressed that he just couldn't do it. She was relatively calm about being left if she had free run of the house and it was his own fault if he hadn't closed the bathroom door to prevent any toilet paper incidents.

He rifled through the drawers in the kitchen, until he found the spare key for the back door.

He rushed to the back door, opened it and then ran back to Orla's side. He carefully slid his hands under her to lift her when she let out a moan. He froze.

'Orla, can you hear me?'

CHAPTER SEVENTEEN

Orla, aged 27. Christmas Eve.

Orla couldn't have been any more bored than she was right now. She'd met Craig online and he seemed nice. They'd spent a few days messaging each other and they got on well, even if it was all online, so they'd decided to meet at a lovely little restaurant called The Tulip Garden on the cliff tops overlooking the sea, the pretty town of Apple Hill Bay and the gorgeous little harbour.

And that's when it started to go wrong. She'd ordered the fried garlic mushrooms to start and that's when he'd started talking about his love of mushrooms. He knew every mushroom there was in the world, or seemingly did; he could identify every mushroom in the wild, which ones were poisonous, which would make you sick and which were delicious to eat. Craig apparently grew his own mushrooms in his shed. He currently had blue oyster mushrooms, pink oyster, grey oyster, yellow oyster, king oyster, and she now knew all the differences. He also grew shiitake, lion's mane, enoki and maitake mushrooms but he really wanted to try growing porcini and truffles because they were apparently the hardest to grow. Orla had never heard the word mushroom so often in a conversation.

Their starters arrived and he insisted on eating most of her mushrooms to see what they tasted like. Inferior was the word he used, especially in comparison to the ones he grew himself. When she asked if she could try his chicken wings, he said he didn't share food and went back to talking about mushrooms again.

She was going to kill Ettie for this. Orla had become really good friends with her over the last three years since they'd started working at Seahorses together. It had been Ettie's suggestion, or rather insistence, that Orla try online dating, berating her for doing nothing but run the café and hang out with her, Fern or Shay all the time. Although it was probably the amount of time Orla and Shay spent together that Ettie had the biggest problem with. Not because Ettie didn't like him – she adored him, but because Orla and Shay were so close, no other man stood a chance. That was Ettie's words. And there might be a tiny bit of truth to that.

She and Shay had slipped back into their old ways so quickly after her return to Apple Hill Bay, meeting most nights on the beach and of course they'd see each other throughout the day because he worked right next door at

The Little Beach Hut Hotel. They were best friends and everyone who lived locally saw them spend so much time together at work and outside of it they assumed they were a couple anyway, so men asking her out were very thin on the ground.

So as Ettie and Fern both had boyfriends, none of which Orla thought would be long term, Orla had reluctantly agreed to widen the net and try online dating. Shay hated the idea, telling her there were too many weirdos out there on the internet, which so far had been true. He didn't like any of the men she had dated so far. She'd stopped telling him she was going on dates now as he always wanted to know everything about them before she went out with them, sometimes making his mind up that he didn't like them without even meeting them. He also always wanted to know when she was home safe, which in this day and age was probably not a bad thing, but it did feel like a crazy one-night stand with one of her hot dates was off the table because of it, not that she'd wanted that with any of the men she'd dated so far.

Just then Shay walked in with his latest girlfriend, Brooke. It was not a total surprise he was there. Apple Hill Bay was so small she'd often bump into him even when she wasn't planning on seeing him. As far as nice restaurants go, there wasn't a great deal of places to go to and The Tulip Garden was well known for its delicious food. Unlike her, Shay never seemed to have any trouble getting a date. Brooke was very pretty with her long dark hair. But none of his girlfriends lasted beyond a few dates. He was clearly looking for something that none of these girls made him feel. She knew that feeling – every time she went on a date with someone, she was always looking for a man that made her feel the way that Shay did, but no one ever came close.

His face lit up when he saw her, and he waved.

'Oh, that's convenient that she's here,' Brooke hissed.

'You chose this place about ten minutes ago, how could she possibly know we were coming?' Shay said.

'She just has a habit of turning up wherever you are.'

'Apple Hill Bay is a very small town.'

'You see her more often than you see me.'

'We practically work next door to each other,' Shay said in exasperation. 'I'm going to say hello.'

'Of course you are,' Brooke said, dryly.

Shay started coming over, with Brooke reluctantly following. That was one of the things all of Shay's girl-friends had in common, they didn't like her, or rather her relationship with Shay, no matter how nice she was to them.

'Hey Orla, how you doing?'

'Who's this?' Craig snapped.

'This is my friend Shay and his lovely girlfriend, Brooke. This is my date, Craig.'

'I didn't know you were on a date tonight,' Shay said, looking over at Craig suspiciously, giving him the once-over to see if he met with his approval. Clearly, by Shay's expression, he didn't.

'First date. Craig was just telling me about his love of mushrooms. He grows his own.'

Brooke snorted and Orla felt bad for Craig, he'd quite clearly heard her laugh at him.

'I've dabbled in growing my own mushrooms too,' Shay said, and Orla smiled with gratitude at him. 'Probably not to your extent, just chestnut and some shiitake. There's something really oddly satisfying about it and it's so easy to do.'

'Some of them are easy, some like the porcini are a lot harder.'

'Yes, I imagine so,' Shay nodded.

'Are we seriously going to stand here and talk about sodding mushrooms all night?' Brooke said. 'I'm hungry.'

'Yes of course, let's go and eat,' Shay said, he turned back to Orla and Craig. 'Enjoy your night.' He looked at Orla and briefly touched her arm. 'I'll see you tomorrow.'

She nodded and they walked away.

'You're seeing *her* tomorrow?' Brooke protested.

'Yes.'

'It's Christmas Day.'

'Yes, I'm aware of that.'

'Why are you seeing *her* on Christmas Day.'

'Because she's my friend and she always comes to my mum's for Christmas Day. She has done since she was fourteen.'

'I want to come.'

'Sorry, it's family only.'

'She's not family.'

'Friends are the family you choose for yourself.'

They walked out of hearing distance and Orla let out a little sigh.

'I don't like him,' Craig said.

'Why not?'

'He wants to get into your knickers.'

Orla choked. 'I assure you that's not the case.' She resisted the temptation of saying, he'd already been there and done that.

'I can tell. He looked at you like he wanted to devour you.'

'I can promise you, sleeping with me is the furthest thing from his mind.'

'You want to sleep with him too.'

Now she couldn't really deny that. 'Shay and I are just friends.'

'Women shouldn't have male friends in my opinion. If things get serious between you and I, you won't be seeing him anymore.'

She suppressed a snort of laughter. There was nothing in the world that would stop her being friends with Shay. What she had with Shay was special and there was no one who could stop her from seeing him.

She looked over at Craig. This was clearly going nowhere. Not only was he quite possibly the most boring man she'd ever met, but the fact he wanted to control who her friends were was a huge red flag. So she could politely endure the evening and never see him again or get out now. She thought about the tub of her favourite mince pie ice cream in the freezer at home and realised she'd much rather be at home eating that than sitting here.

She picked up her bag and put some money on the table to cover the mushrooms she'd barely eaten and the main course that she'd ordered and was no doubt on its way.

'I'm going to call it a night.'

She stood up and pulled on her coat.

'We've not finished our meal yet,' Craig said, clearly shocked.

'I know but I don't think either of us are going to get what we want out of this. Hope you have a lovely Christmas.'

With that she walked out before he could say anything else. She looped her scarf round her neck and walked the short distance to her flat. Christmas lights sparkled from every house and shop and it made her smile, she loved this time of year. She rounded a corner and stopped as there were carollers singing in front of the town fountain. She stopped and listened for a few minutes then dropped some money in their bucket and carried on. There were lots of people doing last-minute shopping, people running past with rolls of wrapping paper in their arms, other people with boxes of chocolates and flowers. Fortunately, all of her presents were wrapped and ready to go.

She let herself into her little flat, turned on the heating and changed into her Christmas pyjamas. She heated up a bowl of her favourite turkey soup which tasted of Christmas and sat down in front of the TV, putting on the Christmas movie channel and finding something gloriously cosy and cheesy to watch.

She loved her little flat: two bedrooms, one that was used to store all her stuff, a tiny lounge diner and a kitchen. She loved the Christmas decorations, the tree laden with purple baubles and trimmings and an abundance of wild animal ornaments dotted around the place wearing various Christmas hats and jumpers.

Her phone buzzed with a text notification. She glanced at the phone and saw it was a text from Shay.

Are you OK? I noticed you'd gone.

She smiled and replied.

I'm fine, the date was a non-starter, so I came home. I'm in my happy place.

She snapped a picture of her feet in her polar bear slippers and the TV with a Christmas movie playing and sent it to Shay.

Looks perfect.

Are you texting me in the middle of your date?

Sort of. I'm texting you from the bathroom so she won't see.

She smiled.

Go back to your date, she seems nice.

That was obviously a lie, but she wasn't going to tell Shay he was dating a moany bitch.

> That's probably a generous assessment.
> OK, I'm going, see you tomorrow x

She studied that kiss for a moment wishing it was something real before she put the phone in her pocket and snuggled down to watch the movie.

Orla woke a while later to a noise. She'd fallen asleep on the sofa; the movie she'd been watching had clearly finished as there was another one playing instead. She looked at her watch and it had just gone half eleven.

What had woken her?

Suddenly she heard another noise, a banging and shuffling coming from her spare room.

She got up and walked towards the door in confusion. Her flat was on the ground floor and sometimes there were cats outside trying to get in – had one of them succeeded somehow, despite her always keeping the windows closed?

She opened the door to see a man standing in her spare room, seemingly looking for something. He was silhouetted against the window so she couldn't see his face.

She screamed, he screamed, she screamed louder and slammed the door. She quickly ran into her bedroom and locked the door then dragged her desk in front of it for good measure. She grabbed her phone from her pocket and called Shay.

He answered the phone on the third ring.

'Hey, you OK?'

'Shay there's a man in my flat, he's just broken into the spare bedroom,' she hissed, though she didn't know why she was whispering, the man already knew she was there.

'I'll be over in two minutes. Lock yourself in your room and try and arm yourself with something heavy to hit him with if he tries to come in.'

With that he hung up.

She stood trembling, straining her ears to listen, wondering if the man was currently ransacking her house while she stood by and let him or whether he'd ran away as soon as he'd seen her. He certainly hadn't been expecting anyone to be home. This was Apple Hill Bay, this kind of thing just didn't happen here. She realised she should have called the police. Maybe she should have called them first, but her immediate thought had been to call Shay as he had always made her feel safe. But just as she dialled the number, there was a noise, which sounded like her front door being opened.

'Orla!'

Relief coursed through her at the sound of Shay's voice. He must have used the spare key she gave him.

'I'm in here, I'm OK,' Orla started dragging the desk out the way of the door.

'Stay in there for a second while I check the place over.'

Surely they wouldn't have hung around once they heard or saw Shay come in. It only took a minute before she heard Shay come back to her bedroom door. 'We're all clear.'

She unlocked the door and threw herself into his open arms. He held her tight and shuffled her back into her bedroom. He sat down and pulled her down on his lap, wrapping his arms tightly around her.

'Oh my god, Shay, I can't believe someone broke into my flat, I've always felt so safe here.'

'The window is smashed in the spare room, but apart from the damage to the window, there doesn't appear to be any other damage. I don't know if he took anything, but my guess is you scared him off before he got the chance.'

'He seemed really surprised to see me. I'm not sure who screamed loudest, me or him. God, I can't stop shaking.'

Shay stroked up and down her back. 'OK, you're coming to stay with me tonight.'

'No, I don't want to leave the house with the window broken open like that. He might come back, or some other opportunist thief might use it to his advantage.'

'OK, then I'll stay here. Tomorrow I'll get some tools and secure it as best as I can with some wood, and you can stay at mine until we can get the glass fixed.'

'OK.'

She climbed off him.

'I'm just going to drag some furniture in front of the window to stop anyone coming back in and then I'll be back,' Shay said.

She nodded and climbed into bed and he left the room. She heard him shifting furniture around and a few minutes later he came back, stripped out of his jeans and t-shirt, so he was just wearing his tight black boxers and climbed into bed next to her, immediately taking her in his arms. She snuggled into his chest. She was still trembling, but she felt that slowly start to fade away as he held her.

'Did you call the police?' Shay asked.

'No, I was so terrified, I didn't even think to call them until after I'd spoken to you. And then you arrived so I didn't get a chance. I'll call them tomorrow.' A thought suddenly occurred to her. 'Oh god, Shay, did I interrupt your date?'

'Ah it's OK. I was starting to wonder what I was even doing with her. I was just trying to think of an excuse to leave her place and go home. Thankfully we hadn't got as far as the bedroom, but I think she was heading that way. Anyway, we broke up.'

'Because of me?'

'Well, she didn't like our relationship, so it was going to come to an end at some point soon.'

'I'm so sorry, I'll call her to apologise.'

'You have nothing to apologise for, someone was breaking into your house and you called me for help. She screamed at me that if I left then we're over, as I ran out the door.'

Orla sighed. 'I don't know if we're ever going to find someone that's comfortable with our relationship. I walked out on Craig because he said if me and him got serious, I wouldn't be allowed to see you anymore. Quite apart from the fact that someone who wants to control who I see is definitely not for me, I'm not losing you for anyone.'

'Well, you know the answer to that problem, don't you?'

'What's that?'

'We should just date each other.'

She sighed wistfully. 'Wouldn't that be wonderful if we both loved each other enough to want to turn our friendship into something more.'

'Yeah, if only.'

They were silent for a moment as she thought how blissfully perfect that would be, two best friends who finally fell in love with each other.

Just then the church clock down the road chimed midnight.

'Merry Christmas Shay, sorry I spoilt it for you.'

'There is nowhere else in the world I'd rather be.'

Orla woke the next morning and smiled when she realised she was still wrapped in Shay's arms.

She looked up at him and saw he was awake. He smiled at her. 'Merry Christmas.'

He kissed her on the forehead and her smile grew even more.

'Merry Christmas.' She studied him as he gazed at her, wanting so badly to reach up and kiss him and start Christmas morning off with a bang.

Just then there was a knocking on the door and she let out a little groan before climbing out of bed.

She opened the front door to find Henry, her new neighbour standing on her doorstep, holding a bunch of flowers. She really hoped the flowers weren't for her, she hadn't even written him a Christmas card. They'd only said hello a few times when they passed each other in the hallway but he seemed nice enough. But flowers were a big step up from passing the time of day.

'Orla, I'm so sorry.'

'What are you sorry for?'

He stared at her in confusion. 'For last night.'

Now she was confused too. 'What happened last night?'

'I broke into your flat.'

'That was you? Henry, what the hell?'

'I'm so sorry. I was drunk, I came home and realised that I lost my key and thought I would just break into my flat. It wasn't until I was standing in your bedroom that I realised I had broken into the wrong flat. Then you came in and started screaming and I panicked and got out of there. I am so sorry. I'll pay for the window to be repaired and any other damages and I hope these flowers will go some way to say how sorry I am. The last thing I'd want to do is scare you, I promise I'm not a weirdo.'

Orla let out a laugh of relief. 'Oh god, Henry, you frightened me to death.'

'I'm so sorry. When I went round the back to break in, I miscalculated which was my window. I can only blame the many pints of beer and possibly the three shots of whiskey. I'm not normally a heavy drinker but it was my birthday and the lads and I got carried away.'

Just then Shay moved behind Orla. Thankfully he'd got dressed.

'Hey Henry, what's up?'

'Oh, hey Shay. I was, erm, just apologising.'

'It was Henry who broke into my flat last night after he got drunk, lost his keys and thought he was breaking into his own flat.'

Shay burst out laughing. 'You idiot, you scared the crap out of us both.'

'I'm so sorry. I said to Orla that I'll obviously pay for any damages.'

'Well, if you know any glaziers that can come out over the Christmas break, that will be great.'

'As a matter of fact, I do. My mate does it and he owes me a favour. I think today and tomorrow will be tricky with all the festivities but I'm sure I could get him to come out on the 27th.'

'If you can do that, then all is forgiven,' Orla said.

'Thank you for your understanding.' He held out the flowers. 'And Merry Christmas.'

He gave them a wave and walked off. Orla closed the door.

'I know Henry,' Shay said. 'He wouldn't have deliberately broken into your house. He's a good man and normally quiet as a mouse. If he says he got drunk and broke in by mistake, then he's telling the truth.'

'I believe him, we've chatted a few times but he's definitely not the type to break into someone's home. I'm so relieved. I don't think I would have ever felt safe here again if that had been a proper break-in. But I feel really bad now that I called you away from your date and it was just a big silly misunderstanding.'

He wrapped his arms around her. 'You didn't know that at the time and I will always be here for you. Always.'

CHAPTER EIGHTEEN

Present day

'Orla, can you hear me?'

Orla's eyes snapped open and she looked up into Shay's concerned ones.

'Oh, thank God,' Shay let out a breath of relief.

She reached up to stroke his face as she suddenly remembered the accident. 'Are you OK?'

'Are you?'

She nodded. 'I think so. But I'm so cold.'

'I know, we need to get you warm. Can you stand?'

She assessed herself; every part of her body hurt but she didn't think anything was broken.

She nodded and with a great deal of effort and with a lot of help from Shay, she staggered to her feet.

She looked around and realised they were outside his

house. Shay must have got her out of the car and up the steps from the beach.

She shivered violently. The skimpy satin dress had seemed a good idea earlier in the evening; she had a coat, but it was in the boot of the car that was currently being washed out to sea. Snowflakes swirled around them landing on her bare skin.

'We need to get inside. I was just about to carry you in when you moaned and I was scared I might hurt you. Can you walk?' Shay said.

She nodded, took a few shaky steps and he wrapped his arm round her, helping her into the house.

'Did you have to break in?' Orla noticed the broken window.

'Yes, my keys are in the car and the spare under the mat was gone. Surprisingly, breaking in was a lot harder than I thought.'

She clung to him. She was shaking so much now and she couldn't stop.

He ushered her inside. The memories of that weekend hit her like a bus. The house was beautifully decorated for Christmas, just as it had been that weekend. It was like opening a door on a memory and walking inside. She could see Shay making love to her on the dining room table, the two of them kissing and cuddling on the sofa, making love in the kitchen after they'd washed up the dinner things. This was why she'd avoided coming to the house all this time – it hurt too much to replay it, knowing it would never happen again.

'Go and get in the shower, I'll call an ambulance.'

'I don't need an ambulance, I just need to get warm and get some sleep,' Orla said.

'We're going to the hospital. You were unconscious for ten minutes, you're wobbly, tired, you've probably got concussion. And they take that very seriously. And so do I.'

'You need to warm up too, you're freezing and soaking.'

'I'll come and join you in the shower in a second.'

He picked up the phone and she didn't have the energy to argue, especially as her head was now filled with the idea of sharing a shower with him.

She staggered shakily into the lounge and saw Ivy fast asleep on the sofa, blissfully unaware how close she'd come to losing her new owner. Orla's stomach lurched with that thought. What if she'd lost Shay in the accident? That thought took her breath away and pain crushed her heart. That was unbearable to think about. She looked back at Shay as he spoke on the phone. He was alive, he was OK, but it could have been so different.

She went up the stairs, kicked her shoes off and walked through the bedroom into the bathroom. She stepped inside the shower and turned on the water.

She couldn't stop shaking as she stepped under the spray with her dress on, and she knew only part of that was from the cold. She rubbed her arms, her chest and her legs under the warm water and it almost stung her skin.

She felt a sob escape her throat and realised she was crying. The shock of the accident had definitely kicked in.

Suddenly the shower door opened and Shay stepped inside, shivering violently too.

'The ambulance might be a while, the snow has caused several accidents tonight. And as we're no longer in the car, they don't deem us to be a priority. We'll get warm and dry and if it's still not here, we'll call a taxi.' He rubbed her shoulders and he frowned when he realised she was crying. 'Are you hurt?'

She shook her head and his face cleared in understanding. He immediately wrapped his arms around her and held her tight as they stood under the spray of the shower and she cried against his shirt. They stood like that for the longest time.

She was still shaking, and still felt so cold.

'Can I get you out of this dress?'

She nodded and turned round, and he carefully unzipped the back. She stepped out of it and turned around, undoing the buttons on his shirt and pushing it off his shoulders as he watched her. The shirt fell to the floor. She rubbed his arms as he stepped out of his trousers, then he took her back in his arms again, holding her tight. He turned the temperature up slightly and steam billowed around them.

'I have never been so scared in all my life,' Shay said.

She looked up at him and he stroked her face.

'I know, falling down that cliff was horrible, I thought we were going to die.'

'That was scary, but I meant seeing you unconscious, I was terrified I'd lost you,' his voice broke. 'I've never felt fear like it.'

'Shay,' she rested her hands on his heart. 'I'm here, I'm OK.' Though she knew she would have felt the same had the situation been reversed.

His breath was heavy as he stared at her. Then he cupped her face and kissed her.

She paused for just a second before she kissed him back. She had no idea what this meant, whether it was just the shock and relief of the accident or whether it was something more, but she didn't care. Right then she needed this.

She wrapped her arms around his neck and pressed herself against him.

Her stomach suddenly rolled and she quickly pulled away from him.

'Sorry, I feel sick.'

'Right, we're going to the hospital now. Get dried and I'll put some clothes on the bed for you. I'm going to get us some transport.'

He turned off the shower, grabbed one of the towels and wrapped it around her, kissing her softly on the head, then grabbed another and walked out into the bedroom.

What had just happened? Although they'd had a tactile relationship ever since they were kids, holding hands or hugging, there certainly hadn't been any kissing – well, not since that weekend. Christ, that kiss in the shower had stirred all kinds of emotions in her, those beautiful, vivid memories, that need for him, her love for him that was still as strong as ever. She couldn't go down that road again – in all those years since, she'd never felt heartbreak like she'd felt when Shay had said he didn't love her. She'd guarded her heart furiously ever since.

She dried herself and her hair, stripped out of her soaking underwear, wrapped the towel around her and walked into the bedroom just in time to see Shay's gorgeous bare bum disappear inside his shorts. She watched him, his back was strong and muscular, as were his huge thighs that were now disappearing inside a pair of jeans.

He pulled on a t-shirt and a thick jumper and turned around, realising she'd been watching him.

He smiled. 'Get dressed, we're going as soon as Theo gets here.'

'Theo?'

'He has a Range Rover, it can cope with the most treacherous conditions.'

'Did you tell him what happened?'

'I told him we were in an accident, but not the details of it, I didn't want to worry him until he can see for himself that we're OK.'

'I really don't need to go to hospital.'

'You really do and we're going even if I have to throw you over my shoulder, cave man style.'

There was something quite sexy about that image and she thought she must be OK if she was thinking things like that, despite the tiredness and sickness.

He left the room and she threw on the clothes he'd left out for her: a pair of his boxers, a thick pair of tracksuit bottoms and a t-shirt and cosy jumper. Everything was massive on her, but at least the tracksuit bottoms had a drawstring to stop them falling down.

She went downstairs just as Shay was answering the door to Theo.

'Hey,' Theo said as he walked in. 'You guys OK?'

'I am, I think Orla has concussion,' Shay said.

Theo looked over at her in concern.

'I'm fine.'

'She's not, she was out cold for ten minutes, she says she feels sick and tired.'

'Christ, what the hell happened? Where's the car anyway? I didn't see it on the road.'

'No, it's probably halfway to France right now or on the bottom of the sea bed.'

Theo's eyes widened in shock and confusion. 'You... went over the cliff?'

'Yeah, there was a deer, I swerved, we skidded and went straight over the edge. We're fortunate that we're not hurt and that we went over at a part that wasn't as steep as some of the others.'

Theo stared at him and then grabbed him in a big hug. After a moment, Shay hugged him back. 'You have no idea how relieved I am that you're OK. I know I don't say it enough, but I love you. And I need you to be godfather to our son when he's born, so no more crappy driving, do you hear me?'

'I love you too, but enough of this soppy bullshit, we need to get Orla to the hospital.'

Theo pulled back and came over to Orla giving her a hug too. 'I'm glad you're OK too.'

She smiled as she hugged him back. 'I'm OK, your brother is just being overprotective as always.'

'He always is when it comes to you. Come on, let's get you checked over and put his mind at ease. Oh, Shay asked me to bring some of Roo's shoes over for you. I have a pair of snowboots in the car.'

'Oh thanks, my sandals are soaked through and definitely not appropriate for this weather.'

'I'll just go and grab them.'

Theo ran back out, leaving the two of them alone and Orla wondered whether they should talk about the kiss and what it meant. He didn't seem fazed at all as he gathered coats, hats and scarves.

'Put these on, you need to keep warm.'

She smiled and shook her head, but she put them on anyway, she still felt a bit chilled.

Theo came back in with a pair of boots and she sat down on the stairs to put them on but Shay knelt down and put them on for her.

'I think I can manage to put on a pair of boots.'

'You need to take it easy, and not make sudden movements,' he said, lacing up the boots for her. He stood up and helped her to her feet. 'Come on.'

'I'll take Ivy home with me until you get out of hospital,' Theo said. 'Ocean will be delighted.'

Theo blew gently on Ivy's head, which was something they all knew to do when waking a deaf puppy. She looked up sleepily, wagged her tail at Theo and he scooped her up and carried her out to the car.

Orla and Shay followed him. Shay opened the back

door for her and she got in and was just fastening her seatbelt when he walked round the other side and got in the back with her.

He put his arm round her. 'Are you warm enough?'

She nodded as she leaned against him.

'Don't go to sleep.'

'I won't.'

'Theo, take it slowly,' Shay said.

'Of course.'

She snuggled into him, knowing that when they got back, they'd really have to talk about that kiss, about all of this.

CHAPTER NINETEEN

December 21st

Orla leaned against Shay sleepily as Theo negotiated the roads back to Shay's house. It was around four o'clock the next afternoon and the snow was still falling heavily, making the whole of Apple Hill Bay look like it was inside a snowglobe, rooftops glittering in the weak daylight. Orla could barely keep her eyes open long enough to appreciate it.

They'd arrived at the hospital the night before. Shay had been hauled over the coals for taking her out of the car until he'd explained that it was either that or let her drown. The hospital had a trauma unit attached and once they'd heard what had happened, she'd been immediately taken to that. When Shay said they took concussion very seriously, he wasn't lying. She'd had a CT scan and despite it coming back fine, they had done observations on her every fifteen minutes, looking in her eyes, moving their fingers in front of her and asking her to keep her eyes on their fingers, shining lights in her eyes, asking her questions about any symptoms she'd been experiencing. Then came the other tests. She'd felt like she was back in school having to recite the alphabet backwards, recall who was the current prime minister and the five preceding prime ministers, memorising a list of words or a sequence of numbers and saying them backwards. There were balance assessments where she had to stand on one leg, walk and turn all with her eyes closed. And then they repeated these tests throughout the night and all that morning. She hadn't been allowed to sleep for longer than ten minutes and she was utterly exhausted.

Shay had had similar tests, despite not getting knocked unconscious in the crash, but they were worried about the trauma caused to his body and brain.

Finally, they'd been discharged with orders for them both to rest and to not be alone for at least the next few days, which was going to be a bit difficult as they both lived alone. Shay had called Theo to pick them up and they were now on their way back to Shay's. She wasn't sure when the decision had been made that she'd stay at his, but she didn't even have the energy to fight it.

Theo pulled up outside Starlight Cottage. 'I'll check in on you tomorrow. I know everyone is worried and wants to come and see you, but I'll try and hold them off as long as I can, give you a chance to get some rest.'

'Yeah, we just need some sleep, we'll call if we need anything,' Shay said.

'Did you want me to keep Ivy for a few more days?' Theo asked, gesturing to the puppy in the boot of the car.

'No, I don't want to confuse her too much as I've only had her a few weeks, so we'll take her now. Besides she's so laidback, she'll just sleep when we sleep.'

They got out and Shay opened the boot and carefully lifted Ivy out and she lolloped off towards the house, frolicking in the snow and finding a branch she proudly dragged around the garden.

They walked back inside the house, waving goodbye to Theo, and Orla smirked when Ivy dragged her branch inside too and Shay clearly didn't have the energy to stop her. He walked into the kitchen and put down some fresh food and water for Ivy, and Orla noticed that the glass in the dining room had been cleared up and wood fixed over the broken window. Theo or probably Fletcher had obviously been round to help secure the house. Once Ivy was sorted, Shay took Orla's hand and led her up the stairs into his bedroom.

He started undressing and she did too. She stripped down until she was only wearing his t-shirt and boxer shorts. When he was only wearing his boxer shorts, he got into bed and then held the duvet up for her to join him.

She hesitated for just a second, the sensible part of her brain telling her she shouldn't do this, that she should insist on sleeping on the sofa downstairs, but she was so tired and sleeping next to him seemed so inviting, so she climbed in. He immediately wrapped his arms round her and she cuddled into his chest. He stroked her hair and she looked up at him.

'You have no idea how relieved I am that you're OK,' Shay said.

He stroked her face and kissed her briefly on the lips, then pulled back slightly, his eyes scanning her face, before kissing her again and despite her exhaustion, she automatically kissed him back.

She pulled back slightly. 'We need to talk about this.'

He nodded. 'Yeah, we do.'

She lay her head on his chest. 'Later.'

'Yes later, I'm not going anywhere.'

She closed her eyes and drifted off to sleep.

Orla woke a while later. It was pitch dark outside and when she looked at the clock, she saw it was coming up to midnight. Shay was still fast asleep.

She was starving – although they'd had a little food at the hospital, it hadn't been much. Her last decent meal had been the buffet she'd eaten at the party the night before.

She carefully climbed out of bed and smiled at Ivy curled up fast asleep in her bed on the floor next to Shay's. She wouldn't wake her. As much as she loved playing with Ivy, puppy chaos at midnight after the stress of last twenty-four hours was not something she wanted to endure right now.

She padded downstairs and looked around. Despite Shay completely redecorating most of the house and replacing all the furniture, the memories of that weekend were still etched on her brain. He'd made love to her everywhere, in the bedroom several times, in the shower, on the sofa, in the kitchen, in the dining room, even against the wall and this was why she'd never wanted to come back. Every corner of this house was filled with those beautiful, incredible memories and it was torture reliving them all again.

She tried to focus on the Christmas decorations, as these weren't the ones that were in the house that weekend. She looked at the garland above the fireplace, filled with real leaves, pinecones and berries. The tree had a collection of white lights twinkling away and just a few baubles. There was one from Ocean, Fern and Fletcher's little girl, there were a few animal-themed ones from the animal rescue he was involved with, there was even beach hut themed ones as he was the manager at the Little Beach Hut Hotel. Her heart leapt when she spotted the bauble she had painted for him as a Christmas gift when she was fifteen. It was of a fox, Clarence, who Shay had sort of adopted after finding him abandoned as a cub. The painting wasn't particularly good and poor Clarence had long since passed on, so why had he kept it all this time?

Her stomach rumbled and she walked into the kitchen to see what she could make. Shay loved to cook, she knew that much, so the cupboards and fridge were unsurprisingly well stocked. She noticed a jar of mincemeat in one of the cupboards so she set about making some mince pies so Shay could have something to eat when he woke up. She spent some time making and rolling out the pastry and that was cathartic, she could get lost in that. She cut out the tops and bottoms of the pies, added the fruity mincemeat which she would normally make from scratch and put them in the oven. While they were cooking, she started making bacon sandwiches for her and Shay. He would be hungry too and she wanted to take care of him like he'd always taken care of her.

Just as she was serving up the bacon onto soft white bread and placing the plates on a tray to take upstairs, Shay appeared at the top of the stairs, looking sleepy and dishevelled and utterly gorgeous.

'Hey, did I wake you?'

'The wonderful smells woke me up.'

'I was just going to bring you breakfast in bed, if you can call it breakfast at one o'clock in the morning. I think our body clocks are going to be a little messed up over the next few days after not sleeping for almost twenty-four hours.'

He came downstairs and peered over her shoulder, stroking a hand down her back which made every nerve in her body come alive.

'Thank you for this. I feel like I should be the one to look after you.'

'You have. You always have.'

His hand was still on her back, and she so desperately wanted to lean into him, to kiss him, to cuddle up to him, but she had to stop this, she was only going to get hurt again. She picked up her plate and walked into the dining room, only to find the table was the exact same table he'd made love to her on. It was a huge oak thing that had a large slab of raw wood on the top. She remembered how she had walked in on Shay admiring it that weekend. She'd told him it was a beautiful table and then he'd kissed her, lifted her on it and then climbed up on top of her and made love to her on it. The memory of it made her stomach clench with desire and need.

She quickly turned around and went and sat in the lounge. At least the sofa was different.

Infuriatingly, he came and sat next to her and took her hand while he tucked into the bacon sandwich with the other hand.

She stared at him incredulously, which he failed to notice. But then her stomach protested loudly that there was food and none of it had made it as far as her stomach yet, so she started eating her own. They sat in silence as they ate, with Shay stroking her hand with his thumb. It was almost as if he needed that physical contact, maybe to reassure him that she was OK.

They finished their sandwiches and he put the plates on the coffee table and then leaned back against the sofa with his arm around her. Her carefully reigned in emotions snapped.

She pulled away from him. 'Shay what the hell is going on here?'

The timer went off on the oven and she sighed and went to retrieve the mince pies which were a gorgeous golden brown.

He followed her into the kitchen. 'You seem angry, are you OK?'

'You kissed me. Twice.'

He shrugged. 'You kissed me back. Twice.'

'That was… nothing. Tiredness, delirium, shock, relief.'

'I don't think it was.'

'What do you think it was?' Orla said in frustration.

'I think you have feelings for me, just like I have feelings for you.'

Her heart thundered in her chest. 'You… you have feelings for me?'

'I nearly lost you last night. When I dragged you out the car I didn't know if you were dead or alive. When I realised you were alive and I was sitting on the beach with you too scared to move you, I kept thinking I'd never told you how I felt, that I'd never had a chance. Of course, I've had hundreds of chances over the years and I was never brave enough to take them. So I swore if we made it through that and you were OK, I'd tell you how I feel. I'm done hiding, Orla. I'm in love with you.'

She stared at him in horror and then walked away from him, her head in her hands. 'No, no, no, this can't be happening,' she muttered to herself. She'd been wanting to hear those words for sixteen years and now she had, she didn't want it.

'That's not really the reaction I was hoping for.'

She turned back to look at him. 'Twelve years ago, I told you I loved you and it ruined everything between us. I was heartbroken you didn't feel the same but the pain of losing my best friend was so much worse. I did that, I threw away the best thing that ever happened to me and now I have you back and I love seeing you every day, chatting with you, spending time with you and I'm not doing anything to risk that again. We're friends, Shay. You're my best friend. I don't want to ruin that.'

There was a part of her brain that was screaming at her for being so stupid. He loved her, she loved him, she should be grabbing him, kissing him and then making love to him again in every single room of the house, including on that spectacular table. But it had hurt so much losing him before, she couldn't go through that again. And how long would this really last? He'd had several girlfriends over the years, none of them had lasted long. And now he'd had this shock of the accident and he was upset at the thought of losing her and he was translating that into loving her, that's all this was. They'd go out for a few weeks or months, she would fall even more in love with him and it would come to an end and she didn't think she could go back to just being friends with him again after that.

'So you don't have feelings for me?' Shay asked.

She turned away from him as she couldn't say that. She couldn't lie to him. 'I think we're better off not going down that road. One or both of us will inevitably get hurt and I don't want to lose you.'

'Orla, I...'

'Shay, I'm really tired. I'm going back to bed.'

He didn't say anything, so she went upstairs and climbed back into his bed. She rolled onto her side facing away from the door. After a few minutes, she heard him come back into the bedroom and get into bed with her, but this time he didn't take her in his arms and she missed that already.

CHAPTER TWENTY

December 22ⁿᵈ

There was a knock on the door later that morning and Shay groaned. He hadn't slept a lot since he'd told Orla he loved her, his mind whirring with everything he should have said and regrets for saying it at all. She had kissed him back – he hadn't imagined that – and he thought that was it, they were going to get together and stop hiding behind past hurt. And while he'd practised saying those words to her many times, and imagined many different ways that it would play out, he'd never envisaged that it would play out like that, with Orla staring at him in horror.

The knock came again and he climbed out of bed.

'That will be my family. Stay here if you don't want to

face them,' Shay said. 'I'll tell them you're resting and try to get rid of them.'

'It's OK, I'd like to see them,' Orla said, sleepily stretching and looking completely adorable.

He threw on a t-shirt and jeans, blew gently on Ivy to wake her up and went downstairs, with Ivy chasing after him and tugging on the hems of his jeans as he walked. He opened the door to be met with not only Carrie and her husband Antonio, but his sister Fern, her husband Fletcher, their daughter, Ocean, their giant Bernese Mountain dog, Bones, Theo, his heavily pregnant wife Roo, their English setter, Clarke and Orla's friend Ettie. So much for rest and relaxation.

He looked at Theo and his brother shrugged. 'I tried. But once everyone found out you stupidly drove your car over the cliff, they all wanted to see you to make sure you're OK and no limbs were missing.'

Shay stepped back to let them in with a sigh. His head was hurting already just at the thought of entertaining everyone. Carrie managed to wrestle her way to the front and threw her arms around his neck. 'I was so worried.'

He hugged her back. 'I'm OK, Mum, we're just tired. The doctors told us to rest so we just need plenty of sleep.'

They all trooped in with Fern giving him a hug too.

'Well you can't be getting much rest here sleeping on the sofa,' Ettie said. 'Orla can come and stay at my house; I have a spare room and I can look after her and you can have your bed back.'

There was an awkward moment where they all looked

over at the sofa to see there was clearly no bedding there. And then to top off the awkwardness, Ivy, who had clearly gone back upstairs to fetch Orla, came charging down the stairs proudly dragging Orla's bra and a few seconds later Orla came downstairs with her hair a tangle of curls looking very much like a woman who'd spent the last few hours having sex, not snoring softly next to him.

'You old dog,' Theo muttered under his breath next to him.

Fern, Roo and Ettie rushed over to give Orla a hug and make a fuss of her.

Carrie hugged her too. 'We're all relieved you're both OK. I don't want you to worry about the café either. I've already put a sign up saying it's closed until the new year. It's high time you took a break, so you concentrate on getting some rest.'

'Thank you,' Orla said.

'And that goes for you too,' Carrie said to Shay. 'We can manage the running of The Little Beach Hut Hotel without you. We don't go on our honeymoon until January so we can take care of everything until then.'

Shay didn't have the energy to argue.

Orla's friends ushered her off to the dining room, while Carrie went into the kitchen to unload what looked like a month's worth of food, which was completely unnecessary. Fletcher and Ocean started playing with the dogs, Ivy, Clarke and Bones, and Antonio sat on the floor and joined them.

Theo looked at him. 'Have you?' he asked quietly.

'No.'

'But you are sleeping in the same bed?'

'Yes, but as friends, nothing more,' Shay said, quietly. He saw Theo's expression of disbelief. 'I honestly don't think it will ever be more than that.'

Theo frowned in confusion. He looked around to see if anyone was listening, but the girls had shut themselves in the dining room and no one else was interested in their conversation. 'What happened?'

'I finally found the balls to tell her I love her. She doesn't feel the same.'

'What? Are you sure?'

Theo knew what had happened between them all those years ago. Shay hadn't told him at the time, in fact it was only a few weeks before that it had finally all come out. Theo was convinced that Orla felt the same. How had they both got it so wrong?

Except he wasn't sure he had got it wrong, not a hundred percent. She had definitely kissed him back.

'Maybe she's still dwelling on the past,' Theo said.

He frowned. 'You think this is her way of getting back at me for telling her I didn't love her.'

Orla was not the type to play games.

'I think you broke her heart, despite her trying to convince you of the opposite. And she's scared to trust you with it again.'

Shay sighed. That felt plausible. Why should she believe that this was something serious for him? He had rejected her once, why would she give him a second chance to do it again?

'Did you tell her that you did love her back then, when you were kids, that you lied?'

Shay shook his head. 'I thought that might make it worse. And if you're right and I did break her heart, she isn't going to be happy to hear that it all could have been avoided if I'd only had big enough balls back then to tell her how I felt too.'

'I think you tell her why you felt like you couldn't tell her the truth. You've had all that counselling, for you and for her, you're a different man now than you were twelve years ago and maybe she needs to see that.'

Shay brushed his hand through his hair. Maybe it was worth a try.

'What's going on?' Ettie said, closing the dining room door behind her as they all sat down at the dreaded table.

'Nothing's going on,' Orla said. She was too tired for this.

'Really, because you and Shay have clearly been sleeping in the same bed and when you came downstairs with just-shagged hair, Shay looked like he wanted to eat you,' Roo said.

Orla cringed at how Fern must be taking all this, her best friend and her brother – it wasn't really appropriate or fair. But Fern simply took Orla's hand. 'Are you OK? Death-defying leap over the cliff and a possible concussion aside, you look really stressed.'

'I do feel stressed, emotional, tearful and a whole

jumble of emotions all vying for attention. It feels like my mind is racing sometimes, as if I can't get my thoughts in order.'

'Honestly, that sounds like a typical concussion,' Fern said. 'Do you remember not long after I moved here, I was riding my bike and I collided with a wall, knocked myself out because I was too cool to be wearing a helmet?'

'Of course I remember. I was there when it happened. You scared the crap out of me. It was the first time I'd ever called nine, nine, nine and I remembered thinking I was going to get into trouble for doing it.'

Fern laughed. 'They printed an article in the local paper saying you were a hero.'

'I didn't feel particularly heroic. The crash hadn't seemed that bad, you weren't going that fast, but you hit the floor like a deck of cards and didn't get back up after that. I had no idea what to do.'

'Physically I was fine, but the doctors were obviously concerned about concussion. I was in hospital for two days before they finally let me go home but I cried for weeks after, for no reason whatsoever. I was anxious and sad and I'd worry over the silliest things. I thought I was going crazy. And I had no idea why I was feeling like this. But Shay did. He loved finding things out in books or on the internet, he loved finding out how things worked and when I burst into tears one day when we were hanging out in the lounge and I cried telling him I was so tired of feeling sad all the time, he went and looked it up – after comforting me of course, he was always a good hugger. To put it simply, concussion can cause inflammation or injure parts of the brain that are responsible for our emotions. We went back to the doctor and he said it was perfectly normal to have that response after an accident and that it would pass after a few weeks, which it did, but he did say talking about what I was feeling or what I was worried about would help.'

She looked around at her friends. They had always been there for each other through every up and down and it didn't feel right to keep this a secret anymore. 'He told me he loves me.'

They all gave squeals of excitement, even Fern. Orla quickly hushed them.

'So you spent a night of passion in his bed?' Ettie said.

'No, I told him I just wanted to be friends.'

They all stared at her in disbelief.

'What? Why would you do that?' Roo said. 'It's plain to anyone that you two are in love with each other.'

Orla sighed. 'We have… history.'

'We're going to need more details than that,' Fern said.

'Are you sure you want to hear it? He is your brother after all.'

'And you're my friend and I want to see you both happy.'

Orla wasn't so sure.

'Is it going to make me think bad things about my brother?'

'No, quite the opposite, he's the hero in this, I'm the asshole.'

'I doubt that, but spill and we'll be the judge.'

So Orla gave them a whistlestop tour of her and Shay's

past, starting with what happened at the party with Kirk, although Roo and Fern knew this as Orla made sure everyone knew what an asshole Kirk was, but none of them knew how it made her fearful of sex, and that made Fern hold her hand tighter when she got to that bit. Orla wondered if she'd still be holding her hand when she told them how she'd persuaded Shay to have sex with her, but Orla ploughed on regardless. She told them all about the glorious weekend here in Starlight Cottage, although she didn't go into the details of how he'd had her butt naked on this very table, but she told them how she'd told him she loved him afterwards and he'd said he didn't feel the same. She told them how she cut him out of her life because of it and how she regretted that more than anything.

'And despite that we're friends now, I've been avoiding coming here ever since he bought the place because I couldn't face all those beautiful memories again, and now I'm here and we've kissed and he's told me he loves me and I don't know what to do.'

There was silence from her friends as they stared at her.

'I had no idea,' Fern said.

'I'm so sorry, I know he's your brother and the thought of us sleeping together must be a weird one.'

'It's fine, I've always felt like you two belonged together and I never understood why you two didn't realise it too. Now all this history explains why you both held back.'

'I can't believe you slept with Shay,' Roo said. 'Was it good?'

'Best sex I've ever had,' Orla said. 'Sorry,' she said to Fern.

Fern smiled and shook her head to show it didn't matter.

'Hold up, can we go back a step?' Ettie said. 'You kissed, recently. Since you've been here?'

'Yes, but it was in the shower, right after the accident, I was upset and he was holding me and we just sort of kissed.'

'You had a shower together?' Roo squeaked.

'We were fully clothed, we were soaking wet after the car ended up in the sea and we were trying to get warm. I think you're focusing on the wrong thing here. Am I crazy for telling him I just want to be friends with him?'

'Yes!' her friends all said at once.

Orla sighed. 'I'm scared of losing him, I'm scared of falling even deeper in love with him and it all ends in a few weeks and what happens then. He's the manager of the Little Beach Hut Hotel, I run the café right next to the hotel reception. We'll see each other every day.'

'You already have to torture yourself by seeing him every day,' Ettie pointed out. 'I'm not sure it will be any different to what it is now, other than you'll have a few more weeks of the best sex you've ever had under your belt.'

Orla couldn't help smiling that Ettie was focusing on that.

'Ettie has a point,' Roo said. 'What's the worst that can happen? You date, he treats you like a queen, going on past behaviour, then you or he decide it isn't working and you call it quits, you'll be upset or he will, you'll have a few weeks of awkwardness and pain but eventually you end up back where you are now, being friends again because you've known each other too long to let it come between you, not now you're older and wiser. And at least you'll know you tried and maybe it will help you move on once and for all. Or what's the best that can happen? Look at me and Theo. OK we never had sex when we were younger, but we were best friends, and when I moved to America and my dad died, I cut him out of my life too. I didn't handle grief particularly well. I came back here fourteen years later and well, eighteen months after that here we are, blissfully happily married with our son on the way in a few months. Isn't it worth the risk to find out if you have that?'

Orla sighed. Maybe they were right. She never wanted to regret the road not taken.

'From a practical perspective, you two are so different to the kids who first made love twelve years ago,' Fern said. 'Shay was so messed up as a teenager, he thought he was worthless – poison was the word he used once. No doubt something his birth parents said to him.'

Orla swallowed down the pain of hearing that. She'd always known his self-worth was in tatters. He was always making comments to that effect. But poison? She hated that he thought that.

'After you left, he told Mum that he wanted coun-selling,' Fern said. 'He said he wanted to stop feeling like he wasn't enough, that it was ruining his life. Looking back now I think some or all of that was for you. He has grown so much in confidence over the last ten or so years. I feel like he sees his worth now. When he was younger, he just couldn't see it. No matter how many times Mum or I or you told him he was loved, and what a wonderful person he was, he never believed it until he was older. Maybe he just wasn't ready for love back then, maybe he needed this time to grow.'

'Do you think... Are you saying he did love me back then?'

'I've always thought he was in love with you, from the moment he met you. And when you came back, five or six years ago, he was over the moon. As far as I can see, he's never stopped loving you.'

Tears welled in her eyes, for the lost years, for what they could have had, but mostly for Shay who had hated himself so much that he didn't think he deserved to be loved.

'It's not too late,' Roo said, clearly guessing what she was thinking. 'I don't think it's ever too late.'

'And you're here for the next few days at least while you recover from your concussion; use that time to talk to him about your fears, about why he said he didn't love you in the past if that's the case. Just be completely honest with him and hopefully he will be honest with you too,' Ettie said.

Orla wiped away her tears. 'Urgh, why are you all so sensible?'

Carrie opened the door and poked her head in. 'Umm

sorry to disturb, but Shay has fallen asleep on the sofa and we thought we'd take off and let you both get some rest.'

'Good idea,' Ettie said, practically leaping up from her seat.

'Yes, these two need to be left alone,' Roo said. 'Erm... to rest, obviously.'

'Call us if you need anything,' Fern said, as she stood and placed a kiss on Orla's cheek.

Orla stood up and followed them out into the lounge as Carrie was ushering everyone out the door. Shay was sprawled out on the sofa fast asleep; he really must be tired if he fell asleep amidst three dogs and a toddler running around.

'Orla dear, you'd be welcome to stay at mine if you want to,' Carrie said. 'Our spare room always has your name on it.'

'Thank you, but—'

'She's fine here,' Ettie said, ushering Carrie out. Ettie gave her a quick hug and closed the door behind them, leaving Orla alone with Shay. And Ivy of course, who was happily chewing on what looked like a pair of Shay's boxer shorts.

Shay looked so peaceful while he slept and so damned beautiful. Her heart broke for the boy he was and for the teenager that grew up thinking he was poison. But maybe she needed to give the man he was now a chance.

She carefully lay down on top of him and he stirred, looking at her sleepily and in confusion. She knew she was sending so many mixed messages here.

'Hey, you OK?' he asked.

She nodded. 'I am now.'

She lay her head on his chest and snuggled into him. He pulled the blanket off the back of the sofa and covered her in it, then wrapped his arms tightly around her and she drifted off to sleep.

CHAPTER TWENTY-ONE

Orla woke a while later and smiled when she remembered where she was, wrapped in Shay's arms.

She looked up at him and saw he was awake. He smiled at her and stroked her hair. Their lips were mere inches apart – if she leaned forward just a little, she could kiss him. His eyes fell to her lips and she knew he was thinking about that too, but he didn't make that move this time. She had said she just wanted to be friends and he was respecting that, although stroking her hair was probably blurring the lines a little, but so was lying on top of him.

'Hey, how are you feeling?' Shay said.

'Still tired.'

'Yeah, me too. But the doctor said that's to be expected with concussion and we just need plenty of rest. I thought I was OK since I didn't bang my head or get knocked out, but she said concussion can occur just from severe jolts to the body. Crashing the car headfirst onto the beach after a two-hundred-foot plummet down the cliff was definitely a big jolt.'

'Yeah, it was. Do you hurt anywhere?'

'Yeah, my back, legs, arms.'

She nodded. 'Me too.'

'I am sorry. Although I'd never want to hurt any animal, I'd never rank the life of a deer more important than yours.'

'What could you have done? If you'd just ploughed straight into it, we would probably have been killed anyway. He was huge, that coming through the windscreen would not have ended well for us. Besides, maybe we should be thanking him.'

He frowned. 'How so?'

'He's given us the opportunity to talk honestly with each other for the first time in... well, probably forever.'

Her stomach gurgled, reminding her they hadn't eaten since their bacon sandwich at midnight, probably thirteen or fourteen hours before.

'Let's get something to eat and then we can talk.'

She tried to get up but found the blanket that was wrapped around her was stuck round her feet. She glanced round to see Ivy fast asleep upside down, legs akimbo, tongue hanging out as she lay on the bottom of the blanket. Orla laughed as she tried to surreptitiously drag the blanket out from underneath the dog in an imitation of the tablecloth trick.

'I think she wanted to be part of the cuddle party,' Shay said.

'And she's very welcome, at least you know where you stand with a dog's affections.'

Shay didn't say anything and she winced. 'Sorry.'

'No that's fair.'

She finally freed the blanket and climbed off him. Ivy opened one eye to look at them and then carried on sleeping.

She wandered into the kitchen and he followed her.

'Mum left enough food to feed a small army. I watched her cramming it into every nook and cranny, but at least we don't need to cook anything, just a quick reheat.' Shay opened the fridge. 'Ah, Christmas has come early, these are her famous roast turkey sandwiches. Shall we take these in the dining room?'

Orla peered over his shoulder. 'Yes, and let's grab some of that cheese and crackers too.'

They took a few minutes to grab some cheese, crackers, grapes, crisps and the delicious smelling turkey and stuffing sandwiches. They also grabbed some glasses of water as well.

They walked into the dining room and she couldn't help smiling at the table. 'Why did you buy this?'

'I made it.'

'What?'

'Remember that four-week course I took with the White Cliff Bay furniture company, when I was sixteen or seventeen? Well, we were all tasked with making a dining table, any size or shape we wanted, and I made this. They had this huge slab of raw, untreated oak propped up inside the factory and they had planned to chop it up and make coasters or something. I asked if I could use it and they said yes. They weren't particularly keen on the idea of not shaping the wood and leaving it like this, narrow at one end, lumpy in the middle, fatter at the other end, but I loved it. And I spent a lot of time sanding down the top and sides so it was smooth and so there was an even surface to eat off, but I kept the raw shape of it. And I was really proud of what I'd achieved at the end. This was the first thing in my life that I'd done that I was proud of.'

'It's beautiful, I love the raw wood effect.'

'I do too. But it's massive, I think it's about twelve foot long. There was no way I could take it home and it certainly wasn't going to be the easiest thing to transport. I told them they could sell it for me. It took over a year for them to find a buyer but eventually they did, although I had no idea who or where it had gone. They gave me five hundred pounds for it. The irony was I used that money to pay for our weekend here and when I walked in here and saw it, I couldn't believe my table had ended up here, of all places.'

'You made love to me on the table you built?'

He grinned. 'Yeah, I did. There was something poetic about that. It made me feel so proud seeing it again and there you were looking at me like a god and for a while – I felt like one. When I realised Antonio had bought it off the previous owner, I had to have it when I bought the house. And if we're being completely honest, making love to you on this table was probably the highlight of that weekend. The whole weekend was utterly spectacular but for some reason this table ranked pretty high.'

She bit her lip. 'For me too.'

He watched her, his eyes going dark with need.

'Stop thinking about making love to me again on this table,' she said.

He laughed. 'I can't help it, you brought it up.'

'We need to talk first.'

'First? So there will be an opportunity to do that later?'

'I guess that depends on this conversation.'

He sat down quickly and she did too. She took a bite of her sandwich and he spread some cheese on a cracker.

Orla looked at the food. 'Let's just eat for a while. I feel like this conversation is going to upset me and I don't want to get too upset to eat.'

'OK.'

They tucked into the food for a while, but Shay kept on passing her worried looks. She felt that way too; this conversation had the potential to change everything. But while they ate, she thought she could at least manage some polite chit chat until they got onto the heavier stuff.

'What are your plans for Christmas?' Orla asked.

'Oh, probably the same as always. Mum, Theo, Fern and the whole menagerie. Although as much as I love them, there's only one person I want to spend Christmas with.'

She smiled. 'Well Carrie has already invited me along to the menagerie as always.'

Most Christmases were spent with Carrie, Shay and the whole family. Sometimes she'd see her parents if they were in town but mostly she'd enjoy the day with her second family.

'Will you see your own parents this year?'

Orla shook her head. 'Mum is in Mauritius with her new husband. My dad's fourth wife has just had a baby, so they want a quiet Christmas with just the three of them. Not that I really wanted to go, wife number four is twenty-three.'

'You're kidding?'

'I wish I was. I know age is just a number, but it still feels weird when Dad's nearly sixty and she's seven years younger than me.'

'Yeah, it is a bit.'

'And it's hardly likely to last with my dad's track record. Every relationship he's had so far, girlfriend or wife has ended because he was unfaithful, so it feels more like he's just sowing his seed rather than actually falling in love.'

'Yeah, some people are just not cut out for relationships. They always think they can get something better.'

And wasn't that the truth. Almost every relationship she'd had had ended because she was always looking for someone who made her feel what Shay had, not just sexually but emotionally too. He'd set the bar impossibly high and no one else could match that. Maybe Roo was right, if she did get together with Shay and it didn't work out, maybe she needed this time with him for closure, to finally move on once and for all.

Ivy came in the room, dragging one of Shay's boots with her, making them both laugh. She knew Shay had spent a long time puppy-proofing the place so anything chewable was out of reach, cushions put away in cupboards, things like cables hidden away behind screens or cages he'd attached to the walls so she couldn't chew through a cable and get an electric shock, but it was easy to forget that things like toilet roll or boots were hugely tempting to a five-month-old puppy. She looked so proud of her little self as she thrashed it around.

Shay grabbed a bag of treats and offered one out to her, signing the word 'drop'. He had started teaching her various words in sign language so he could communicate with her, but it was going to be a long road. Fortunately, she was very treat driven and was more than happy to swap the boot for a treat. She ran off with a big smile on her face and came back a few seconds later dragging a roll of kitchen roll.

Orla laughed. 'She's so full of mischief.'

'Oh, she's like this all day. Thankfully I can bring her to work with me and she loves greeting all the guests. I normally take her for a walk in the mornings and that wears her out, but with all the sleeping and recovering we're doing, she's missed out on that today and now we're paying the price of unspent energy. I'll take her out for a walk later.' He repeated the sign for 'drop' and offered out a treat and she took it. He followed her out to the lounge and Orla watched as he grabbed a few toys and engaged her with dragging them across the carpet for a few minutes as Ivy chased them. She pounced on a long fluffy octopus toy and started chewing that and while she was distracted with that, he came back to finish his food.

Finally, they finished their meal and Shay took all the plates back to the kitchen before returning to the dining room. Her heart fluttered with nerves about what they were going to talk about, but she was going to be brave and take this step with him – she would always regret it if she didn't.

She looked at him as he sat back down. 'Yesterday, I said I just wanted to be friends because I'm scared of losing you. Cutting you out of my life was the hardest, stupidest thing I've ever done and I never want to go through that again. I would rather have you in my life as just my friend than not have you in my life at all. So you have to promise me that no matter what happens, we'll be OK.'

He didn't hesitate. 'I categorically promise. There is nothing that will stop us from being friends. I don't want to lose you either, not again. This, whatever it will be, it won't change us. First and foremost, you will always be my best friend.'

'OK. I have to know something and it's going to kill me if you say yes, but I have to know. Did you love me? That weekend, when I told you I loved you, did you love me?'

'Yes. I'm sorry, I wish the answer was different, I wish my feelings for you only developed in the last few years and I could have a clean conscience, but I did, I loved you so much. I have always loved you.'

Emotion clawed at her throat and tears filled her eyes. Tears for them, for him. It was all so needless.

'I'm so sorry,' Shay said. 'I hurt you and I can't ever take that back. I've done a lot of crappy things in my life but the one thing I regret more than anything is looking you in the eye and telling you I didn't love you, especially when it wasn't true. I ruined everything between us.'

'No, I did that, I was young and so in love. It was so black and white to me back then, I couldn't be with you so I couldn't see you again.'

'I broke your heart.'

She nodded. 'Yes, you did. And I've had several relationships over the years, the break-ups never hurt as much as ours did. Love never felt like how I felt for you either, not even close. But I should never have pushed you away.'

'I get why you're wary of getting involved with me again. I broke your heart once, why would you trust me not to do it again?'

'Because you're a good man, the very best. I've always seen the good in you. Even when you couldn't see it yourself.' She reached out and took his hand. 'Why did you say you didn't love me?'

He shook his head and absently stroked the grains of the table with his other hand. 'My birth mum always said she wished she'd never had me, that things had started to go wrong between her and my birth dad when she got pregnant with me. Apparently, my dad used to hit her when I cried as a baby, because he was annoyed with the noise, or he'd hit her when there was a mess in the house or when she was just too exhausted for sex. She blamed it all on me. One of the first memories I have was falling over in the garden and cutting my knee and crying and her shouting at me saying she hated me and wished she'd never had me.'

Tears filled her eyes and spilled over her cheeks. 'Shay, I'm so sorry.'

'As I grew up, she was always telling me Dad hit her because of me, it was my fault. She said I was poison and that everything I touch, everyone I came in contact with would be ruined. She said no one could ever love me because I was such a vile, horrible child. You get told it enough times, you start to believe it.'

He pushed his hand through his hair. 'I never felt I deserved to be loved. When Carrie adopted me, I thought she must be stupid because why the hell would she want me? Even after the adoption papers came through and it was all final, I still kept thinking she'd change her mind when she realised what kind of person I was. Fern and Theo were different, they'd both been through crappy childhoods too, so I can understand why they bonded with me, but you, I never understood why you wanted to be my friend. I felt like I was contaminating you just by being near you. You always saw the good in me, no matter what. I yelled at your parents, swore at them actually, and you kissed me on the cheek and hugged me. I punched your ex-boyfriends for laughing at you over you freaking out over sex and you held the hand that was bruised from fighting and stroked it. I always felt like I was ruining your life by being with you, that I was dragging you down, holding you back.'

He sighed and looked at her. 'When you asked me to sleep with you, I couldn't get out of my head that I was... sullying you with my filth. That's why I originally turned you down, but then I thought about you having your first time with someone who wouldn't treat you with the respect and care that you deserved and I thought maybe for the first time in my life I could do something good, that I could make your first time something lovely.'

'You did, it was completely perfect. All my friends at the time said they never really enjoyed sex – even Fern said her first time was pretty rubbish – but you made it so special for me, not just the first time, every time.'

'I got carried away that weekend. When I originally said yes, it was only going to be a one-time-only thing. I only booked the weekend to give you time to relax and be comfortable with it and if you freaked out, we would have time to try again. I never envisaged a whole weekend of sex, or that you would want that. But our first time was so utterly glorious that I wanted more. And when you wanted that too, I couldn't turn that down. That weekend you looked at me like I was some kind of god and for a brief moment, I started to believe that maybe I was worth something. You're smart, brilliant, kind and I thought if someone like you liked someone like me, I must have something good going for me.'

He shook his head. 'When you told me you loved me, it was honestly the happiest moment of my life and then all that fear and doubt and self-loathing kicked back in. I was never going to be good enough for you, I could never give you the life you deserved and if we were to go down that road of marriage and children, I would ruin your life and probably our children's life too. So I said I didn't love you and I have regretted it every day since.'

Orla wiped the tears away. 'You put me on a pedestal that was impossible to reach.'

'Funnily enough, my counsellor said the same thing.'

'Tell me about the counselling.'

'I was so angry after you left. I'd lost the best thing that ever happened to me because I couldn't get past all that fear and hatred. It was a huge wake-up call for me. I looked at all my relationships, especially those with my family and realised they weren't where I wanted them to be. I couldn't just tell myself what I was feeling was nonsense, it was too ingrained for that, so I asked my mum to help me get some counselling. Mum being Mum, she never asked why, she just sorted it out for me. My counsellor helped me realise that what I have is a pretty good package.' He smiled. 'I told her I wanted to be a better man for you and she said I needed to work on being a better man for myself first.'

'And she said you'd put me on a pedestal?'

'Yes, which pissed me off because at that point I thought you were perfect.'

She smiled. 'You don't anymore?'

He grinned. 'We all have flaws and baggage; my counsellor helped me to see that I could love you with all your warts, not pretend they didn't exist. She made me write a list of all your bad qualities, which was hard, let me tell you – that took many weeks to even come up with five. But once I did, I could see that me and you were similar in many ways, the good and the bad. She made me see that if I could love you with all your flaws, which were so similar to mine, then why couldn't I love myself?'

She smiled at that. 'I like your counsellor.'

'It wasn't an overnight change. I had counselling for five years until I finally reached a place where I felt like I didn't need it anymore. But yeah, the self-loathing is gone.'

'I'm pleased you're in a better place now.'

'But?'

'No buts. I think that moment when you said you didn't love me has had an impact on our friendship ever since. I've always held myself back from getting too close, not wanting to come here to your house because I didn't want to face the memories of that perfect weekend and how it ended. And I think in my mind I never let go of the boy who turned me down, even all these years later. I never gave the new improved Shay a chance. But now I think I'd like to.'

He watched her carefully. 'What does that mean?'

She got up and sat on his lap. 'I'd like to be more than friends.'

Then she kissed him.

Feelings erupted in him as soon as their lips touched and he wrapped his arms around her. Pure joy exploded in his heart. He was going to get a second chance with her. Christ, this kiss was something else. In the shower it had been a desperate need to feel she was alive, a kiss born of relief and shock. But this was a kiss of love and desire and need, of years of missed opportunities. She tasted divine. He stroked her face, ran a hand gently down her arm, then slowly traced his hand round her waist. She was definitely more woman than the girl he'd made love to when she was eighteen, and he loved it. He wanted to touch her all over, rediscover her body all over again, but he knew he had to take things slow. Just because she wanted to give them a chance, didn't mean she wanted to jump straight into bed with him. They should date first, do it properly. She pressed herself up closer against him and as he moved his hand to her neck, he accidentally grazed her breast. She gave a little soft gasp against his lips.

'Sorry, believe it or not, that was an accident.'

She giggled, took his hand and placed it firmly back on her breast before kissing him again. So much for going slow. He ran his hand across her breast, feeling her nipple press through the thin fabric of his t-shirt she was wearing. She gave a soft moan and desire and need for her flooded through him at that sound.

He stood up and lifted her onto the table, cupping her face and kissing her hard. She pulled at his t-shirt and he stopped kissing her for just a second as she yanked it over his head. Her hands on his chest was the most incredible feeling in the world.

He pulled on the drawstring on the tracksuit bottoms she was wearing. They were done up so tight to stop them falling down it took a few moments longer than he wanted to undo them but finally they were undone and she lifted her bum to help him pull them off. He didn't waste any time and dragged the boxer shorts she was wearing down her legs too, then he kissed her again, sliding a hand up her legs. The feel of her was wonderful and she moaned softly as he touched her. He pulled back slightly, watching her. Her breath was heavy, her eyes were dark, she leaned her forehead against his, clinging to his shoulders.

'Shay.'

His name on her lips as he sent her over the edge was such a massive turn on, as were the moans and whimpers of pleasure. He needed to be with her now. He pulled off her t-shirt and kissed her neck, running his mouth over her breasts as he pushed his jeans and shorts off.

He moved between her legs, but she suddenly put a hand out to stop him.

He looked at her in concern, was it moving too fast for her?

'Sorry, I'm not on the pill anymore.'

He let out a little sigh of relief. 'I have condoms in the downstairs bathroom.'

'Then why are you still standing there?'

He quickly raced from the room, glanced at Ivy who was fast asleep on top of her octopus toy, ran into the bathroom, grabbed the box and ran back through the lounge to get to the dining room, he suddenly stopped as a thought occurred to him. He grabbed a cushion off the sofa and ran back to the dining room to find her perched naked on the side of the table, exactly where he'd left her. She looked in confusion at the cushion.

'Well, the doctor said you need to be gentle, no sudden head movements. I figured banging your head on a hard table might not be the best thing for it.'

She smiled and wrapped her arms around him. 'How

did I get so lucky to find someone so kind and thoughtful?'

'I'm the lucky one.'

She reached up and kissed him and the kiss was so sweet, that he put the box and cushion down, wrapped his arms around her and kissed her back.

CHAPTER TWENTY-TWO

Orla stroked her hands across his chest and shoulders; he was so gloriously strong. She couldn't believe this was happening. Two days ago, she was happy because she'd managed to have a dance with Shay. Now they were about to make love on his dining table and not because she'd persuaded and coerced him to do it, but because he loved her, because he'd always loved her. Tears pricked her eyes again because she was so damned happy right now, she felt like she could burst.

She pulled back slightly and he stroked her face. She caught his hand and pressed a kiss to his palm. Then she shuffled back, tugging on his hand to follow her. He climbed up on to the table and she lay down. He crawled up her, placing a kiss on her stomach, trailing his hot mouth up towards her heart where he lingered lovingly before moving over her and kissing her softly on the mouth. She stroked the back of his head.

He pulled back, grabbed the cushion and gently lifted her head, placing the cushion underneath. She smiled with love for him.

He pulled a condom from the box, ripped it open and then looked back at her. 'You still doing OK?'

She smiled and nodded.

He moved back over her, and she wrapped her legs around him and with his eyes on hers, he moved carefully inside her. He let out a groan of need as he sank deeper inside her. 'Orla, I love you, I love you so damned much.'

She wrapped her arms around him and kissed him and he started moving gently against her. She knew it was cowardly, but she couldn't say it back. She wanted to trust in him, she wanted to believe this would be forever, but her poor damaged heart was too scared to go all in yet. If she didn't say it out loud it felt like she was protecting herself.

Every movement was slow and exquisite, somehow making her feel things she'd never felt from another man. She loved how much care he was taking with her as well, even after all this time. He was always such a gentleman. And while she didn't mind sex that was fast and hard, he was probably right that she needed to take it easy after the accident. Besides, slow, gentle sex with the man she loved was utterly wonderful.

He moved his mouth to her neck and she stroked a hand through his hair, gasping at the feel of his hot mouth on her skin. She had dreamed about doing this again with him and it was already far surpassing any fantasies she'd had about him. He stroked a hand across her breast and she felt that feeling coiling in her stomach, that tightening that ignited every nerve, every cell of her body, as he took her higher and higher. She clung to him as she soared, shouting out his name and she felt him fall over the edge too. He collapsed down on top of her, his breath heavy against her neck. Then he pushed back to look at her and she could see the love he had for her in his eyes and although she didn't say the words, she knew she still loved this man and impossibly, after their conversation and after this, she'd fallen in love with him a little bit more.

Orla was lying sprawled out on top of Shay's chest as he ran his fingers up and down her back. They'd lay on top of his table for a while after they'd made love, just kissing and stroking each other, rediscovering each other's bodies after all this time. Then they'd made it back up to his bed where he'd made love to her again. She couldn't be any more blissfully happy than she was right now.

She looked up at Shay and smiled when she saw his face reflecting her own happiness. He looked at her and gave her a sweet kiss.

'I can't believe we're here after all this time,' Orla said.

'I know, I can't believe it took us a near-death experience to get us here.'

'Yeah, we really needed an honest conversation before now. I read all these romance books where I get really infuriated by the characters not talking to each other, as it would save them a lot of heartache. But in reality, people never do – they protect themselves, deal with hurt by running away from it, avoid confrontation as much as possible, they never have the big chat. Maybe those books I read are closer to reality than I thought.'

'In my defence, I did try to have that conversation with you when you came back, that night on the beach when I told you I'd had counselling. But then you said you hadn't loved me, you were young and confusing the emotions of sex with love and that you only loved me as a friend.'

'Oh god, I was trying to save face, make things less awkward between us. If you didn't think you'd broken my heart then we could be friends again without you creeping around me feeling bad for me.'

He stroked her face. 'I get it, I do. But if I'd told you I loved you that night, would you have given me a second chance?'

'Back then? Probably not. I'd carried that hurt with me for six years. I don't think I could have thrown myself into your arms, I had to learn to trust you again. Maybe we needed this time to grow.'

'Maybe.'

She shuffled up him and cupped his face. 'None of this is your fault. You can blame your parents for all this. They made you believe you weren't worth loving. People like that should never be allowed to have children. But I'm very glad they did, because I get to have the most incredible man I've ever known in my life.'

He smiled and she kissed him.

She pulled back and looked out the window. It was

dark outside, but the snow had stopped falling, though it was still covering the ground like a glittering blanket.

'What time is it?'

Shay checked his watch. 'Just gone five.'

'I feel like I'm losing all track of time since the accident, I don't even know what day it is?'

'Monday, 22nd December.'

She snuggled into his neck and then sat up. 'The boat parade. We were going to go.'

'Theo will understand if we don't. If you're too tired, we can stay here.'

'I'd like to go.'

'We can still go. It doesn't start until seven. We've got time.'

She grinned. 'Time for what?'

'Well, we should probably have a shower.'

'Together?'

'Is there any other way?'

CHAPTER TWENTY-THREE

Orla smiled as she walked down to the harbour, the town looking so pretty wrapped in a glittery blanket. There were Christmas lights everywhere. People's houses were lit up inside and outside with trees, lights, dancing snowmen on the lawns or Santas on their sleighs, stars sparkled in the windows and around the doors. Some had gone all out with festive flamingos or peacocks, which didn't seem that Christmassy but somehow worked. The shops looked spectacular with their window displays twinkling and showing off their festive wares.

She looked up at Shay, who was holding her hand. Her heart felt so full of him. She couldn't be any happier right now. Ivy lolloped by his side, chewing on the lead, stomping through the snow, trying to catch the snowflakes.

The harbour was surrounded by strings of multi-coloured lights and many of the boats were decorated and lit up too. Theo had organised the boat parade to help raise money for Little Paws, the wildlife animal sanctuary he owned. All the passenger boats that ordinarily did coastal tours, wildlife or dolphin spotting trips in the summer had donated their boats for the night for people to watch the procession of sailing boats, and tickets to go on board had sold out with all the proceeds going towards Little Paws. Other locals that hadn't made it onto the boats lined the long breakwater that protected the harbour from the waves and storms, to see the procession from dry land, and they'd paid an entrance fee to enter the breakwater too. There were stalls set up too, selling Christmassy goods and foods with a percentage of their sales going towards Little Paws.

As they approached the hordes of people joining the queue for the boats, she spotted Roo, Theo and their puppy Clarke. Roo waved and as her eyes fell on Orla and Shay's joined hands, a smile filled her face. Ivy launched herself at Clarke, squealing in delight. Roo came hurrying over and gave Orla a big hug, which caused her to drop Shay's hand for a second, and Roo used the distraction to her advantage, linking her arm and walking her away from Shay. Orla looked back at Shay helplessly and he just smiled and shook his head – he knew what her friends were like.

'What's going on?' Roo said, making sure Shay was no longer in hearing distance.

'We're here to see the lights,' Orla said, innocently.

'You're holding hands.'

Orla relented, partly because her friends should know,

and partly because she was so happy she wanted to shout it from the rooftops. 'OK, we had a big honest chat, told each other everything and we're giving it a go.'

'You're dating?' Roo squeaked excitedly.

Orla smiled. 'Yeah, we are.'

'Oh wow, I'm so happy for you. I always thought you were made for each other. I think pretty much everyone has been waiting for you two to realise it too. This is so exciting.'

'We're taking it slow,' Orla said, knowing that wasn't exactly true since they'd already made love three times since the chat, but what she actually meant was that she was taking things slow by trying to hold back her feelings for him, which didn't seem particularly fair as Shay had already told her he loved her twice now.

'Well, maybe don't tell Carrie – she'll be planning the wedding before the New Year.'

Orla wondered what Carrie would make of it. She'd known Orla as long as Shay had – she'd practically been a second mum to her. Would she think it was weird that they'd got together after all this time? How would she feel if she ever found out that Orla had persuaded Shay to sleep with her when they were younger, or that they'd had a whole weekend of sex? Would she look at her differently? Carrie had never asked Orla why she had cut Shay out of her life either. Would she be happy that they were finally together or would she worry that Orla would hurt Shay again?

She bit her lip as she thought. She *had* hurt Shay, probably as much as he'd hurt her. It wasn't just Shay that had to prove he wasn't going to hurt her again, she had to prove that too, that she wasn't going to run away again at the slightest hint of trouble. They certainly had a lot of baggage and history to get past if they were going to have any kind of future.

'I can see that frown, what are you worried about?' Roo said.

'I'm not.' Orla silently cursed that Roo knew her so well.

'Just enjoy it for what it is now, stop worrying about the what ifs and the future.'

Orla nodded. 'I definitely intend to enjoy it.'

Roo laughed. 'The fun stuff, the excitement, the thrill, and let's face it, the sex, is always the best part in any new relationship. Embrace it, relish in it. You've waited a very long time for this, wring out every last drop of joy from it. And then if it ends you can look back on it with fondness, not regret.'

'You're right of course, you always are.'

They looked back at Shay who was chatting to Theo.

'Come on, let's get some hot chocolate and let them have a chance to talk. I hear there's a stand over there that sells churros too,' Roo said.

'Well, I'm definitely getting some of those.'

'Well, how's it going with Orla?' Theo asked after Shay had deliberately got Theo talking about the boat parade to try and distract his brother from the incoming inquisition.

He focused on Ivy and Clarke playing together for a moment while he played for time. He wanted to talk about it – God knows he could probably do with some advice from his brother about it – but he also wanted to protect what he and Orla had. It was so new and it still felt so tentative. He dreaded the idea of their mum finding out because he knew she would go completely over the top with her enthusiasm. When Fern had been dating Fletcher, Carrie only had to get a whiff of an impending proposal for her to march Fern down the wedding dress shop and insist on buying her a dress. He really wanted to protect Orla from that.

'We talked, honestly, probably for the first time ever. She did love me when we were younger, I did break her heart, which I hate, but at least we're starting from a place of truth and hopefully we can move forward from that. She's decided to give us a chance.'

'Mate, I'm over the moon for you. I know this has been a long time coming but you really deserve this happiness.'

Shay smiled. 'I can't tell you how happy I am. I've been in love with her for sixteen years, but I've always been too scared to make a move, especially after what happened in the past. And now we're together and it seems... unreal. I'm almost expecting her to change her mind.'

Theo frowned. 'Why would she change her mind? She loves you too.'

'I think so. She's not said that yet. I told her again

while we… were cuddling and she just kissed me, she didn't say it back.'

'It's still really early days for you two. I know it doesn't feel that way when you've known each other and been such good friends for so long but this is all new, so you have to take your time. I knew I loved Roo the first time we made love, but I never told her that for at least a week, might have been a bit more. I didn't want to scare her off. And with what happened the last time Orla told you, I'm not surprised she's holding back. She needs to know this is something big and life changing for you, that you're in it for the long haul, that it won't end in a few weeks. I think deep down she knows that, but you have to give her time to trust in it.'

'What can I do to get her to trust me?'

'Just give her time. She'll soon realise how important this is to you. In the meantime, just enjoy your *cuddling*.'

Shay laughed. 'I intend to.'

CHAPTER TWENTY-FOUR

Orla and Roo walked back to Shay to see that he and Theo had been joined by Fern, Fletcher, Ocean and Bones. They were all chatting and laughing together. The dogs were all happily playing together. Shay looked really happy and she smiled at the thought that she might have had something to do with that.

His face lit up when he saw her and as she approached, he looped an arm around her shoulders, she wrapped an arm around him and he kissed her on the head. She quickly looked to see what everyone's reaction was to this show of affection, but everyone clearly knew, as none of them looked shocked, only happy for them.

'Well, we'll see you both on the boat,' Fern said, ushering everyone away clearly to give her and Shay some space.

He bent his head and kissed her and she smiled against his lips. 'You taste sweet.'

'I had churros. I did save you one, but Roo stole it.'

'That's OK, I can always get my own.'

'Did you tell them about us?' Orla asked, gesturing to their departing friends and family.

'They kind of guessed. Theo saw us holding hands and Fern said I was glowing with happiness. You don't mind, do you?'

'No, not at all. I'd already talked to the girls when they came round. They were the ones that persuaded me to go for it and stop being a big scaredy cat.'

'Then I'm eternally grateful to them.'

Ivy grabbed hold of Shay's scarf and tried to tug it from him. He took it off and dangled it around for her to catch and chase. Orla couldn't help smiling at the puppy's antics.

'If it helps, I'm scared too.' Shay went on. 'I want this to work more than anything. I love you. And I'll tell you every day until you believe it. And I will understand if this doesn't tick the box for you. It's been twelve years since you loved me, I'm not expecting you to have held onto those feelings for me all this time, just because I have. So if in a few weeks or months you decide you don't want this anymore, I'll understand. But for me, I'm in this for the long haul.'

She leaned up and kissed him. 'I just need some time. This feels like it's come out of the blue a little. I had no idea you felt this way and I need to get my head around us in a relationship and not just friends anymore.'

'There's no rush. I know I hurt you and I have to earn your trust again, in that regard.'

She stroked his face. 'I hurt you too when I ran away, after everything you did for me, not just that weekend but throughout all our years of friendship, I showed you that friendship was expendable. We both have some baggage we need to get past but if we can, then this will be something serious for me too. Just give me some time and let's enjoy the now.'

He smiled. 'Wise words.'

He bent his head and kissed her.

'Oh my god!'

Shay swore softly.

Orla pulled back to see Carrie and Antonio walking towards them, Carrie had the biggest grin on her face as if she'd just been told she'd won the lottery.

'You're dating? I had no idea. How long has this been going on? Why didn't you tell me? There's me inviting you to stay at my house earlier today and you two were secretly together.'

'We weren't dating,' Shay said. 'Not then. We are now.'

Carrie's face lit up. 'This is all brand new? I'm so happy for you, for both of you. I could see how important you were to each other even back when you were kids. I always felt like you had a special relationship, I'm not surprised it's turned into something more. Oh, how wonderful. Isn't it wonderful?' Carrie said to Antonio.

'It is, of course,' Antonio said, clearly looking amused by Carrie's reaction. Carrie obviously wanted more than that. 'Umm, congratulations.'

Orla smirked. 'Thank you. We're very happy.'

Carrie clapped her hands together in excitement. 'And

what's wonderful about dating your best friend is you don't have to spend weeks finding out if you fit with each other, you already know that you do. It's almost too easy. And without all that second guessing, you can bypass all that dating stuff, which is purely to get to know each other and go straight for the serious stuff. I expect you'll be getting married soon, or at least getting engaged.'

'Mum, it's been eight hours. I'm not asking her to marry me after eight hours of dating,' Shay said.

'Well, no, that might be a bit quick, but you don't have to spend months fannying about either, that's just a waste of time. You need to get your wedding or registry office booked sooner rather than later as these things get booked months in advance.'

'Mum…' Shay started.

'And I saw the cutest little wedding outfit for Ivy the other day in one of the shops in town. Of course you'll want to involve her in the wedding too. I should have bought it. I'll see if it's still there tomorrow.'

'Why don't we go and find Theo,' Antonio interrupted. 'There's been a lot of planning for tonight and I'm sure he would appreciate knowing we are here to support him.'

'Oh yes of course,' Carrie said. She came over and gave Shay and Orla a big hug. 'We can talk about all this later.'

Antonio quickly ushered her away leaving them alone.

'I'm so sorry about her,' Shay said.

'Don't be. She loves you and she wants you to be happy. And talking about weddings doesn't scare me off. She's right, if things go well for us – and by that I mean longer than eight hours' track record – that will be the next step for us.'

His face split into a huge grin. 'That would make me so happy.'

'Not yet though, let's not get too far ahead of ourselves.'

'Of course, we should wait at least ten hours.'

She laughed. 'Come on, we need to go and get on the boat.'

He took her hand and they walked down towards the little jetty where people were already boarding the boats. They handed over their tickets and boarded a boat that had been renamed, at least for this evening, the Snow Princess. The boat held around forty passengers and once it was full, it left the dock and made its way a little out to sea, along with the five other small passenger ferries and sightseeing boats. The boats themselves were decorated with lights and one of them even had a fully decorated tree stuck to the top.

The boats bobbed around in the sea for a bit and Orla shivered as she stood against the railing waiting. Shay moved behind her and wrapped his coat around her, holding her close against him, and she smiled as she leaned back against him. She suddenly wasn't cold anymore.

Ivy poked her head through the railings of the boat as if she was excited for the parade too.

There was a cheer as the procession of sailing boats left the inner harbour and Orla leaned forward to get a glimpse of them. This had been a massive undertaking and Orla knew so many people from Apple Hill Bay had contributed to this. It had been a big community project.

The sailing boats all glided towards them. The first boat sailed past with the title of the story, *The Christmas Wish*, projected on its sail. Orla knew Theo had written the story and he and Roo had animated it themselves, She knew it was the story of a little boy asking Santa for a friend, although she didn't know much more than that.

What followed was basically a short, animated film, with each sailing boat projecting a ten-second clip on its sails. The first one showed a little boy looking sad and lonely in his bedroom. The second clip and boat showed him writing a letter and throwing it up the chimney. The third one showed the letter travelling through the skies, clouds and stars as it made its way to the North Pole.

The animations were cute and beautifully done and she could see people were completely enchanted with the story as the boats drifted past.

The boats showed Santa in his workshop, the elves busily making the toys, the reindeer playing football in the snow, which made everyone laugh, Santa receiving and reading the note, the elves busily loading the sleigh for Christmas Eve including a special box that sat next to Santa as the sleigh took off, the lid of the box coming off and a puppy poking his head out. Santa tucking him into his jacket to keep him safe, Santa visiting various cities and sights around the world with the puppy taking it all in with wide-eyed excitement before he was finally placed under the tree of the little boy and curled up and went to sleep.

It was a gorgeous story and the boats looked so beautiful as they glided past in a long procession. Everyone cheered and clapped as the last boat drifted past. Even Ivy barked with all the clapping and excitement.

'That was wonderful,' Orla said.

'It was. Theo and Roo have been working hard on it for months.'

She turned round and looped her arms around his neck. 'I'm glad I got to watch it with you.'

He smiled and kissed her. 'I think we'd planned to watch it together anyway, although there certainly wouldn't have been any kissing or cuddling.'

'I like it better this way.'

'I do too. Come on, let's go and find Theo and Roo and congratulate them, then I can take you home.'

She smiled at the use of the word home, even if he didn't mean it like that.

They joined the others in a queue to get off the boat and waiting at the top of the jetty was a small stall handing out mince pies, glasses of mulled wine and cups of hot chocolate. Orla took a hot chocolate and passed Shay one too.

They spotted Theo and Roo with Fern and Fletcher although lots of people were coming up to congratulate them.

They made their way over and Roo hugged them both.

'That was wonderful, the story, the animation, the boats, it was all beautiful.'

'Thank you,' Theo said. 'The designs were all Roo.'

'But you took care of the animation side of things,' Roo said.

'Well it worked brilliantly,' Shay said.

'Thank you,' Roo said. 'We're very proud of it.'

'I think we raised over five thousand pounds too,' Theo said. 'Probably more once we take a percentage from all the stalls.'

'That's great, what will the money be used for?' Fern said.

'Some new incubators for the baby animals that come into our care, and then just general upkeep,' Theo said. 'Oh, excuse me, we must just go and thank some of the boat owners.'

He and Roo rushed off.

'Listen,' Fern said to Shay. 'You were supposed to be looking after Ocean tomorrow morning, but if you're not feeling up to it after the accident, we can try to find alternative arrangements.'

Shay looked at Orla, which was sweet to include her when it wasn't really her call to make, but she nodded anyway.

'That's absolutely fine, we'll be happy to have her.' Shay stroked the back of Ocean's head as she was snoozing on Fletcher's shoulder. 'I've got some activities planned anyway, so it's no bother.'

'It will only be a few hours,' Fletcher said.

Orla nodded. 'You know I'm always happy to spend time with her.'

'Thank you,' Fern said. 'Can we give you two a lift home?'

'That would be great. I really need to sort out some kind of transport, but it's probably easier to just wait until after Christmas now,' Shay said. 'And I have some things I need to take care of at home too so it will be good to get back sooner rather than later.'

'No problem.'

They started walking back to the car with Fern and Fletcher a little way in front and Ivy bouncing along at their side.

'What do you need to take care off back at your house?' Orla asked.

Shay fixed her with a dark look. 'You.'

She smirked and grabbed his hand and hurried to catch up with Fern.

Sitting in the back seat with Shay wedged in next to a sleeping Ocean in her baby seat, Orla felt like a giddy teenager again. Shay had his coat draped over her legs to keep her warm, but it was his hand on the inside of her thigh that was making her all hot. It was far enough down her leg that he wasn't going to make her spontaneously combust in the back of Fern and Fletcher's car, but close enough to make her heart race. He stroked the inside of her thigh and she looked at him. He gave her a wink, knowing full well what he was doing to her.

It had only ever been him that made her feel this way. Even back when they were kids, before they made love and she had all these seemingly unrequited feelings for him, she was always looking for a boy that made her feel the way she felt when she was with Shay, that giddy, excited, happy, joyful feeling. Of all the men she'd dated over the years, no one had ever come close to giving her that. And here she was, all these years later, and those feelings had never gone away, and in fact over the last few days they seemed to have intensified into something so much more.

'Orla, I could stop by your flat on the way to Shay's tomorrow morning, pick up some clothes if you want,' Fern said from the front seat. 'You can't live in Shay's clothes forever.'

'No, probably not,' Orla said, although she knew Shay got a big kick out of seeing her walk around in just his shirt or t-shirt. 'That would be great. You still have my spare key, don't you?'

'Yes I do.'

'Just grab some jeans, t-shirts and jumpers, oh and some underwear, that would be much appreciated.'

'No problem. How long do you think you'll be at Shay's for?'

Orla fell silent. She couldn't just move in with him, it felt like it was way too soon for that, but right then she was far too happy to want to go home.

Fern must have read her mind. 'Concussion is a serious thing. It's probably best if you have someone staying with you for at least another week, just to be safe. I'll get enough clothes and underwear for a week and if you need more, I can always go back and get more for you.'

Orla smirked at the not-so-subtle interference. 'Thank you.'

They went round a corner and Orla fell into Shay a little, which caused his hand to shift higher up her thigh. He still wasn't touching where she needed him, which was a good thing, but she let out a tiny whimper of need and he had the audacity to smirk.

The car pulled up outside Shay's house and Orla quickly got out.

'Thanks for the lift,' she said.

'Yes thanks,' Shay said, climbing out too.

'We'll see you tomorrow about ten,' Fletcher said.

'Yes, great,' Shay said, lifting Ivy from the boot where she was snuggled up with Bones. He waved goodbye and ushered Orla up the drive.

Fletcher drove off and Shay quickly unlocked the door, bundling Orla inside. The door wasn't even closed before he kissed her hard.

Clothes came off very quickly until they were just in their underwear. Orla laughed to see Ivy running off towards the bedroom, dragging Shay's jeans behind her. Her laughter turned to a gasp as his hands started exploring her body hungrily as if he couldn't get enough of her. He was insatiable and she loved it. The kiss continued as he removed her bra and his hands immediately encased her breasts, stroking them, caressing them until she was whimpering with need. He shuffled her back against the door and then trailed his mouth down her throat, over her chest and across her belly, then knelt down on the floor. He slowly peeled down the boxer shorts she was wearing, his eyes on hers the whole time. But there was no preamble this time, no building up to it, he kissed her right where she needed him the most.

'Shay!'

She ran her hands through his hair. His kiss, his touch made her feel weak. It was everything. He knew her better than she knew herself. He very quickly took her roaring over the edge, leaving her gasping for breath. He stood back up and she kissed him, sliding her hand into his shorts. She could feel how much he wanted her. She moved her hand slowly over him and he groaned against her mouth. He caught her hand and lifted it to his mouth, kissing her palm.

'You keep touching me like that, baby, and this is going to be over very quickly.'

She smiled and kissed him, pushing his shorts down, and he kicked them off.

'Where do you want me?' Shay whispered against her mouth. 'I'm yours, do whatever you want with me.'

She kissed him, shuffling him backwards until his legs hit the back of the sofa and he sat down.

'Right there.'

He quickly leaned over and grabbed a condom from the little side table drawer. He had scattered them everywhere earlier like some sexy version of the easter bunny. She had laughed at his forethought, but she was grateful for it now. He quickly slid it on and she straddled him; with his hands on her hips he guided her down on top of him. She kissed him as he moved deep inside her, letting out a moan against his lips.

She started moving against him and he matched every move perfectly, his hands around her lower back, holding her tight against him. He moved his hands up her spine, stroking her, caressing her hair as it tumbled down her back. He kissed her throat, her breasts and she felt herself going higher and higher, that glorious feeling spreading through every inch of her body. She kissed him as that feeling exploded through her, moaning hard against his lips. He held her tight against him as he found his own release, making noises that sounded almost like a roar.

She pulled back to look at him, trying to catch her breath, and though she didn't say the words, she hoped he knew that she loved him with everything she had.

CHAPTER TWENTY-FIVE

December 23rd

There was a knock on the door the next morning and Shay rushed to answer it. Bones, Fern and Fletcher's giant Bernese, burst into the house first, tail wagging excitedly, big smile on his face. He greeted Shay and then bounded over to greet Orla who also gave him all the fuss and attention he needed. Ivy launched herself at him, wrapping her paws round his neck and nibbling at his ears.

Fletcher walked in carrying a sleeping Ocean on his hip and Fern brought up the rear carrying a bag which was presumably Orla's clothes, which made him smile. He knew it was early days for them and he didn't want to rush her, but it felt so right having her here. It should have felt weird having someone living in his house, sharing his bed, but she was meant to be here.

'Hey, how are you two feeling?' Fern said, handing Orla her clothes.

'Better, not so tired anymore, still a bit achy but we did get jolted around in the accident,' Orla said.

'Yeah same, just a bit stiff,' Shay said.

'Well, take it easy, don't feel the need to charge around with Ocean, I'm sure she will be happy to just sit down and do some craft activities,' Fletcher said.

'Well, that's what I'd planned, at least to start with. And maybe if we have time, we can make a snowman too,' Shay said.

'Oh, she'll love that,' Fern said. 'Here's Bones's phone.'

Shay smiled at that. Bones was diabetic and his blood glucose levels were transmitted to his phone which Fern carried around everywhere so she could see what his levels were doing. It was all very clever, but it did make Shay laugh that Bones had his own phone. He checked the level to see Bones was at a very healthy ten and slid the phone into his back pocket. The alarm would go off if Bones went below a certain level, so he didn't need to worry too much.

Fletcher handed Ocean to Shay and his niece stirred. She looked at Shay for a moment in confusion then her eyes lit up, a big smile filling her face.

'Say,' Ocean said in delight.

'Hello princess.'

She wrapped her arms around him and gave him a big hug.

'Thanks for doing this, we should be back in two hours,' Fern said.

'It's no bother.'

They waved goodbye and left.

He turned round to face Orla and she came over to greet his niece.

'Hello Ocean.'

'Ola.' She held out her grabby hands for Orla and Orla took her from his arms and gave her a hug.

'We thought we could make some Christmas cookies first, do you want to do that?' Orla asked, carrying her through to the dining room.

'Cookies,' Ocean squealed in delight.

'I'll take that as a yes,' Shay said as he followed them. Cookies had been received far more favourably than he or Orla. Bones and Ivy came trotting into the dining room too.

The table had been covered in an attempt to protect it, but Shay knew, based on previous cooking attempts with Ocean, that flour and other ingredients ended up *everywhere*.

Orla placed her down so she was standing on a chair and put an apron on her before putting one on herself. Shay quickly put one on too, though he knew it would do very little to stop the mess. After one particular cooking adventure with Ocean, he'd found icing sugar inside his boxer shorts.

Orla, being a baking queen, had already premeasured out all the ingredients into separate bowls. Shay was more one to chuck everything in and roughly guess how much was needed, especially when cooking with his niece.

'So first we are going to mix the butter and sugar

together. Do you want to add these two ingredients to the big bowl?'

He loved the way she talked to Ocean – there was no cutesy baby talk, she just explained everything clearly and Ocean seemed to understand, even if she couldn't communicate it. She probably had around fifty words in her repertoire, and was starting to join some words together, like 'no sprouts' or spats as she called them, or 'more juice', 'more cake', and 'more coclot' were some of her favourite phrases.

'That's it, use the spoon to scrape the butter out... or your hand works just as well,' Orla said, suppressing a laugh as Ocean got butter smeared all over her hands in seconds. Not wanting the sugar to feel left out, Ocean also used her greasy hands to swipe the sugar out of the bowl too, coating her hands in sugar that stuck to the butter. Ocean clapped her hands excitedly, then rubbed them together, obviously enjoying the texture and the friction rubbing her hands was causing.

'Mummy and Daddy are going to be delighted when we hand you back,' Shay said.

Ocean let out a squeal of laughter as if she agreed.

'Now we're going to mix the sugar and butter together,' Orla said, handing Ocean a wooden spoon which she used to bang on the table.

Shay laughed. He was used to this, but he didn't think Orla had done any baking with Ocean before, although she had babysat for her a few times, so maybe she had. Orla seemed unfazed as she grabbed another wooden spoon. She banged it a few times on the table to join in with Ocean, and then started mixing the butter and sugar together, redirecting Ocean to the task without saying a word. After a few seconds, Ocean started helping with the mixing, even if a lot of the sugar ended up on the table as a result of her helping.

'That's great, Ocean,' Shay said. 'You need to make sure all the sugar is mixed in so it's nice and creamy.'

Although it was quite clear that Ocean was having more fun flicking the sugar everywhere than actually mixing it.

'I'm not sure how good these cookies will taste when half the ingredients are going to end up on the table,' Shay said.

'In true *Blue Peter* fashion, I have a batch of cookies I made earlier so we can decorate and eat those,' Orla said. Ocean sneezed in the bowl. 'My cookies might be more hygienic too.'

Shay laughed.

'Now we need to add this egg,' Orla said, passing Ocean the beaten egg.

Ocean poured the mixture in and it splatted into the bowl, which made her giggle. Abandoning the spoon, Ocean decided to mix the ingredients together with her hands, mulching the egg and buttery mixture through her fingers, and as she did, the bowl tipped up and half the mixture fell onto the table, and splatted over Ocean, Orla and Shay, which Ocean thought was hilarious.

'Looks like we'll both need a shower after this,' Shay said, picking some eggy butter out of his hair.

'Oh, that's your game, is it?' Orla laughed, wiping her face.

'Any excuse to get you in the shower.'

She smiled and shook her head. She scooped as much mixture as she could back into the bowl and helped Ocean to mix it together, although throwing it on the table had already partly done that. Once it was mixed, Orla moved two smaller bowls towards Ocean.

'Now we add the flour and the baking powder. Do you want to add these two bowls to the big bowl?' Orla said.

He smiled as he watched Ocean tip the flour and baking powder into the bowl from a great height. Predictably, quite a bit landed on the table.

'Good job,' Shay said, and Ocean let out a giggle as she rubbed her eggy, buttery hands in the floury, eggy mess on the table, making some kind of slime.

Orla carried on mixing the ingredients together, but Ocean was far too busy enjoying spreading the ingredients out all over the table.

'Want to scoop out the cookie dough, like this,' Orla showed Ocean, using an ice cream scoop to spoon up the dough and put them on the baking tray where she flattened it slightly. She handed Ocean the ice cream scoop and she banged it on the table a few times as if testing it out and then copied what Orla had done scooping up the dough and sticking her tongue out as she tried to get the dough on to the baking tray.

'Perfect,' Orla said. 'Right, I'll go and put these in the oven and when they are done, we can decorate them.' Orla picked up the baking tray and carried it off to the kitchen.

'And me and you can wash up all these bowls,' Shay said to Ocean. Her eyes lit up. She loved washing up possibly more than she loved making cookies – anything to do with water and she was there. Shay stacked all the bowls and utensils together, scooped Ocean up with one arm and the bowls in the other and followed Orla through to the kitchen.

She was already filling the bowl up with warm soapy water with possibly a bit too much soap, which he knew Ocean would get a big kick out of. She loved playing with all the bubbles. He placed the bowls down, grabbed a stool and dragged it over to the sink and stood Ocean on it. She plunged her hands straight into the water and squealed with laughter when the bubbles flew everywhere. Water sloshed over the side and onto the floor and Orla quickly grabbed a few tea towels and lay them down on the floor in an attempt to catch some of the water. Ocean clearly thought the whole thing was hilarious. She slapped the water, splashing it everywhere as the bubbles floated around the room.

Shay stood behind her and with his hands round her, started washing up the dishes. There was next to no help from Ocean as she just kept on playing with the water. Intermittently, between each bowl, he joined Ocean with splashing the water and she squealed in delight. He started singing, *Splish Splash,* which he'd sung to her many times before and he laughed when she started joining in, obviously not singing the lyrics, but humming along as she splashed.

He realised Orla was watching him and he looked at her and saw she was smiling.

'You're so good with her. Have you thought about whether you want children of your own?' Orla asked.

'I have. For a long while I never wanted that because I thought I would ruin any child's life that would be unlucky enough to have me as a dad. Plus, I had terrible parenting role models, and I always worried I might end up like my dad and I definitely didn't want my children to go through what I did. But the counselling made me realise that I had a lot to offer a child of my own and I realised that my crappy upbringing would actually ensure that my children would never go through that, I'd make damned sure of it. I could be a better man because I knew I deserved more than what I got and my children deserve better too. And when Ocean came along, it was really easy to be there for her, to look after her and love her and spoil her rotten, and yeah, it made me want kids too. One day, when the time is right.'

Orla smiled at that.

'What about you?' Shay asked as he continued to splash in the water. 'You didn't have the greatest childhood either with your parents arguing all the time, does it put you off marriage and children?'

'No not at all, I've always wanted children. As an only child, I've always wanted brothers and sisters, so I'd like to have a few kids so they can be there for each other like the relationship you have with Fern and Theo. And no, my parents fighting hasn't put me off marriage. Like you said, I know I can do better. Choose the right man to start with, someone I can trust to be loyal and love me forever. Someone I can talk to honestly if there are problems in the relationship and who will talk to me too so we can grow to be better together.'

'Yeah, you saw the worst of a marriage and I think it gives you a better idea of what not to do,' Shay said.

She smiled. 'When I was younger, I always used to dream about what it would be like to be married to you. It's funny, in my fantasies, we were always living here, sitting on the beach every night or in our garden overlooking the sea, putting the world to rights, just like we did back then. I never thought it would come true, but it was a nice dream.'

He focused his attention on washing up a bowl. They had missed out on so much, so much wasted time and lost opportunities, but they were here now.

'Maybe one day, I can make that come true for you,' Shay said.

He glanced at her and she smiled. 'Maybe. One day. And for what it's worth, I think you'll make an excellent dad whenever you do have children.'

He smiled at that as he turned his attention back to the washing up, but he couldn't help hoping it would be with her.

Orla watched Shay dress Ocean in what seemed like a hundred layers to go outside. She had two scarves and two hats on as well as gloves and wellies. Anyone would think they were dressing to go for a walk at the North Pole. Fresh snow had fallen again overnight, and the garden lay untouched, glittering in the early morning sunshine.

Orla pulled on her own hat as they stepped outside. Both Bones, being a Bernese Mountain dog and Ivy, a Newfoundland, were born for the snow and they charged out to enjoy it, seemingly determined to leave their pawprints on every inch of the garden. She smiled as Shay took Ocean's hand as they walked over the snow. It gave her a lump in the throat. It was weird to think about all those dreams she had about her future when she was a teenager; getting married to Shay, living here, having children with him, and until that glorious weekend she never thought they ever stood a chance of happening. Then he'd made love to her, and with the way he'd held her and adored her, for the first time she'd suddenly believed it could all actually come true until the weekend ended so badly. And here they were all these years later, together, here, happily in love, and it was hard to believe it wasn't all just a dream. But it was now hers for the taking if she was only brave enough to do so.

'We're going to make a snowman,' Shay said, kneeling down to Ocean's height. 'You might have seen pictures of snowmen before.'

'Olaf,' Ocean said, excitedly.

'Yes, exactly. We're going to make an Olaf. Only ours won't talk and walk.'

Ocean didn't seem to care or understand that as she started flicking her hands to make the snowman just like Elsa did in *Frozen*.

'No, we have to make ours with our hands,' Orla said. 'We don't have magic like Elsa.'

Orla bent and scooped some snow together to make a large ball and then started rolling it around the garden to collect more snow, packing it tight as she rolled so it didn't come apart. She noticed Shay doing the same and Ocean eventually gave up flicking her hands in the hope of magic coming out of them and joined Shay by adding tiny handfuls of snow to his ever-increasing snowball. He rolled it up so it was standing just outside the patio doors and then came over to lift Orla's large snowball on top of it.

Bones came over to inspect the strange creature before bounding off to enjoy the snowy garden again with Ivy.

'Shall we make a smaller one for the head?' Orla suggested.

'Good idea, your ball is way too big for a head.'

Orla laughed. 'I got carried away.'

'Carried away? He'll look like some kind of ogre if we make this the head. It's also not particularly round, more like a flat oversized rugby ball, definitely not head-shaped. Are you trying to scar my niece for life?'

'I'm trying to teach her that people come in all shapes and sizes and that it's OK to have an oversized rugby ball as a head. Besides, if you want to be accurate, there is nothing anatomically correct about snowmen: he has no legs and feet, and twigs for arms.'

'True.'

Orla looked down at Ocean to see she was mirroring Orla's own body language, her arms folded across her chest indignantly, even if she didn't know what she was indignant about. 'See, even Ocean agrees with me.'

'OK, OK, rugby ball heads are perfectly acceptable for a snowman. But I still think this one needs a separate head, purely so he has a good height.'

'OK, Ocean do you want to help me build a head?'

Ocean bent down and scooped up the world's tiniest snowball in her hands and offered it out to Orla. She suppressed a smirk.

'Maybe just a little bit bigger,' Orla said diplomatically.

'I thought all shapes and sizes were equally important,' Shay said.

'I don't think we'll get a carrot or button eyes in that.'

'Fair point.'

Shay started rolling up a small snowball for the head and when he was done and lifted it into place, he carefully added Ocean's offering on top, which Ocean seemed happy with.

'OK, now for the accessories,' Shay said. He rushed back inside and came out with a box. 'This is my snow-man-making kit, we have a big pink scarf, a hat, buttons and of course the carrot.' He picked Ocean up and passed her the scarf and with a little bit of help, she wrapped it around the snowman's neck. She took the top hat and placed it on his head at somewhat of a jaunty angle, which added to his charm.

'Now we need two buttons for the eyes,' Shay said, pointing out approximately where the buttons should go. Although it seemed Ocean had her own ideas where the eyes should go, placing them right in the middle of the face and at a very wonky angle.

'Perfect,' Shay said, and Orla smiled.

'Now use these smaller buttons for the mouth,' Shay said.

Ocean giggled as she placed the buttons in a diagonal line that made the snowman look very puzzled.

'Good job Ocean,' Orla said. 'He looks great.'

'Olaf,' Ocean said and started humming, 'Do you want to build a snowman?'

Shay put her down and she ran off to play in the snow with Bones and Ivy.

'She's very musical,' Orla said.

'Yeah, I think Fletcher and Fern sing to her all the time.'

They looked over at her and she was making handprints in the snow.

'Hey, Ocean, want to make snow angels?' Shay said.

She nodded, probably with no idea what she was nodding to.

'A very wonderful woman taught me how to do this,' Shay said, and Orla smiled.

Shay went over and lay down in the snow and started moving his arms and legs outwards and inwards. Ocean watched him for a moment and then lay down and copied him exactly, making a tiny angel compared to his giant one.

Bones and Ivy bounded over to see what was going on. Ivy rolled over on her back as if she wanted to make a snow angel too. Ocean giggled at this.

They stood up to admire their art and Ocean laughed and pointed, Orla wondered if she was laughing at the size difference too.

'Right, Ocean, shall we go and decorate those cookies now?' Orla said.

Ocean clapped her hands together and charged into the house.

Orla smiled as she followed her back in. Shay came back in, stamping his feet as she helped Ocean to get out of her outside clothes. Orla and Shay took off their coats, hats and boots too before chasing after Ocean who had already disappeared off to the kitchen.

Orla filled the sink with warm, soapy water and dragged the stool back to the sink, then lifted Ocean onto it. 'We need to wash our hands first.'

Ocean didn't seem to have a problem with this as she plunged her hands back into the warm water, splashing water everywhere. Orla gave her hands a quick wash too. Then Shay moved behind them both and put his hands in the water as well, which made Ocean laugh and made Orla lean back into him, enjoying his solid warmth behind her for a moment. He kissed the back of her neck while Ocean was busy playing with the water and Orla smiled. She turned round in his arms and with Ocean still distracted, she kissed him, stroking his face.

'Kiss!' Ocean shouted and Orla turned round to see that the little girl was watching them.

Shay laughed. 'Yes, kiss. And kisses for you too,' he scooped her up and started peppering hundreds of kisses over her face as Ocean squealed and giggled in delight. He carried her out the room and into the dining room and Orla gathered the cookies and all the paraphernalia needed to decorate them, then she followed them through to the dining room.

'What do you want to put on your cookie?' Orla asked Ocean as she placed the stuff down on the table.

'Olaf!' Ocean said.

'I should have seen that coming,' Orla said.

'I'm going to do a Christmas tree on mine,' Shay said.

'Kissmas tree!'

'Do you want to help me do mine?' Shay asked.

Ocean nodded as she sat down next to Shay. Bones came into the room and sniffed the air appreciatively.

'No cookies for you my friend, that would send your blood glucose way too high,' Shay said.

Bones flopped down in a corner as if he understood he wasn't getting any. Ivy came in and cuddled up next to him.

'So first I'm going to do a tree shape on my cookie with this green icing,' Shay said as Orla quickly decorated a cookie with a basic snowman shape so Ocean could add the hat, scarf, nose, eyes and mouth once the snowman shape had set.

'Now we can add the baubles and other decorations to the tree,' Shay said. 'Do you want to use Smarties for the baubles?'

Ocean nodded keenly. Shay grabbed the little bowl of Smarties and handed it to her. Ocean very carefully took one and placed it on top of the tree and then grabbed a large handful of Smarties and smushed them into the green gooey icing. Orla snorted with laughter.

'Well, that's definitely one way to decorate a tree,' Shay said.

'I'm not sure it even looks like a tree anymore.'

Ocean giggled loudly as if she knew it wasn't a tree but didn't care.

'She's certainly won the award for most Smarties used on one cookie,' Orla said.

'I don't know, I think she could fit a few more on there,' Shay said. Ocean obliged by adding another handful. 'Yes, apparently she can.'

Orla laughed. 'I dread to think how many Smartie eyes the Olaf cookie is going to have.'

'Olaf cookie,' Ocean held out grabby hands.

'Please,' Shay reminded her.

'Peas.'

Orla passed her the cookie, which she inspected for a few moments, where Orla imagined she was planning her artistic masterpiece, but instead of decorating it, she took a massive bite.

Shay burst out laughing. 'Maybe she thought it was already decorated beautifully enough and there was no need to improve on perfection.'

'Maybe eating the cookies is far more exciting than decorating them.'

'You're probably right.'

Just then there was a knock on the door.

'Ah that will be Mummy and Daddy come to collect their wayward child,' Shay said.

Shay went to open the door and Bones charged off to greet them as if they'd been gone weeks not just a few hours. Orla quickly gathered a few cookies for Ocean to take home and for Fern and Fletcher to have, then she scooped up Ocean and took her back to the kitchen to clean her hands one more time, so she was semi-respectable for going home, although there was definitely some kind of food in her hair. After her hands were clean, Orla carried Ocean back through to the lounge where Shay was chatting with Fern and Fletcher.

'Here are some cookies we made.' Orla handed over the Tupperware container.

'Thank you,' Fern said.

Ocean took a few moments to show her parents Olaf in the garden before goodbyes were said, Ocean and Bones were bundled out the door and they were left in silence.

Shay took her in his arms and kissed her. 'Thank you for your help today.'

'It's no bother, I enjoy spending time with Ocean.'

'Do you think we'll make good parents, or will our children be spoiled rotten?'

Orla didn't know how to answer that question. It was one thing to talk earlier about whether they each wanted children and marriage in the future, but something else to talk about their own children like it was a foregone conclusion. But of course, she wanted that, she wanted this thing between them to work, she wanted marriage and kids, she'd been wanting that with him her whole life. But she was scared to trust in that future right now, she felt like she was protecting herself by not believing in it. That way if it all came to an end in a few months' time, she could walk away unscathed. But she knew it was too late for that. She loved this man, and she was falling deeper in love with him every second she was spending with him. There was no protecting herself from getting hurt from this.

She cleared her throat. 'I think *if and when* we do have children, it will probably be a bit of both. Those kids will be loved so much, so naturally that means being spoiled, but hopefully we'll be good parents too.'

'I think so. Having two parents who love them and love each other is the best start we can give them.' He looked at his watch. 'Come on, we need to leave soon if we're going to get to the Christmas market before it closes.'

He kissed her on the forehead and walked off into the dining room to start clearing up.

Orla watched him go and she couldn't help feeling they'd taken another step forward in their relationship with that conversation, while her heart was still holding back.

CHAPTER TWENTY-SIX

Orla looked at the cute wooden cabins that had been set up on the village green for the Christmas market and couldn't help smiling. Everything looked so festive. The snow that had fallen over the last few days still lay in a thick blanket on top of the rooves and more snow was gently falling now, adding to that Christmassy feeling. Everything sparkled, not just from the glittering snow but from the festive lights that twinkled from the eaves and the splendidly decorated Christmas trees that were interspersed between the huts. There were garlands of holly and berries hanging from the roofs of each hut too. There were ice sculptures decorating the green as well, or what appeared to be. Orla suspected they were made from glass or resin as they certainly didn't show any signs of melting. But whatever they were made of, they were impressive. Sparkling statues of elves, snowman, reindeer, polar bears, Santa and his sleigh all festooned the area in the middle of the green.

She looked up at Shay, holding her hand as they walked around. He made her so damn happy. She glanced down at Ivy who was also looking up at Shay adoringly. Orla wondered if Ivy had any idea what a wonderful life she was going to have with this kind, brilliant, generous man who saved her.

There were stalls selling candles of every scent where Orla spent a few minutes sniffing all the Christmas ones like *frosty dawn, angel* and *toffee apple*, a stall selling churros and crepes, one selling baubles of every colour and size and covered in cute Christmas characters, there was one selling funny festive village paintings, another selling mulled wine, one selling chutneys and jams, one selling wooden sculptures. Orla knew she could spend hours looking at all the gorgeous festive offerings.

One stall even had festive dog treats, which of course Shay bought for Ivy.

She stopped at one stall to look at some antique jewellery. A lot of it was marcasite which she loved because it seemed to have a perpetual twinkle while still capturing that vintage style she loved. She picked up an owl pendant that had a turquoise belly and green crystal eyes and the rest of the body, wings and head adorned with marcasite. It was beautiful.

She ran her finger over the belly feeling the coolness of the stone and looked up at Shay watching her.

'A lot of your jewellery has this kind of vintage style. Do you prefer that over the more modern styles?'

She loved that he'd noticed that about her. 'Oh yes, I love it, especially the 1920s, art deco styles. They were real statement pieces.' She picked up a pendant that had a large bluey purple cabochon in the middle surrounded by swirls of silver, crystal and marcasite. 'This kind of thing was very popular back then and for me, I don't think this kind of style ever goes out of fashion. I'd wear this with jeans and a t-shirt. Anything with a long drop, like an elongated teardrop was also very popular and I love that too. But I also love the modern takes on antique jewellery. Something like this owl or this beautiful kingfisher wouldn't have been in style back then, but it still has that gorgeous vintage feel. Anything with marcasite is a winner for me, but also, I love the pops of colour from the turquoise or amber.'

'Are you going to get something?'

'Oh no, with the café being closed over the last few days and the countless Christmas presents I've bought, I couldn't afford it right now, but that's OK, I probably have enough jewellery to open up a small stall myself. I've amassed quite the collection over the years, mostly bought from car boot sales or charity shops, I probably don't need any more jewellery. It's just nice to look at it.'

She inspected a few more pieces and then glanced over at Shay to see what he was looking at. Her heart leapt to see him looking at the selection of engagement rings. Surely, he couldn't be thinking about proposing to her just yet. It had only been a few days and everything still felt so new and precarious. Although maybe that feeling of precariousness was coming from her not him, but still, it was way too early for marriage and proposals. Although from his point of view he already knew every single thing about her. As Carrie said, they didn't need to take the time to get to know each other or find out if they fitted, because they knew they did. Maybe this was his way of showing he was all in on their future.

No, she was being silly, he was not going to propose. There was lots of jewellery over there besides the engagement rings; he could be looking at potential gifts for Fern or Carrie. She laughed to herself at the panic she'd started to feel at the thought of him proposing. She wondered what she would do if he did. Her heart would scream yes because she had been waiting for that for almost her entire life. Her head would be more cautious because if it came to an end now, she would be heartbroken, but if it came to an end six months or a year into marriage, she would be devastated. Staying friends after a failed marriage would be even harder to do.

But fortunately, she wouldn't have to worry about any of that because he wasn't going to propose. She'd not even told him she loved him yet, although of course she did, but surely he would wait for that at least.

Realising she was watching him, he stepped back away from the stall.

'You ready to go?'

She nodded and took Shay's hand as they walked off to the next stall which was selling snowmen dressed as every occupation imaginable; astronauts, doctors, fire fighters, police, bakers, car mechanics, pilots were just a few that she spotted.

They wandered on, passing stalls selling Christmas decorations with a coastal vibe, festively decorated cupcakes, Christmas pyjamas and Christmas fused and stained-glass decorations. Shay bought a few things from a few stalls. She bought a candle for Ettie.

'Oh, I've left my gloves somewhere,' Shay said, patting down his pockets. 'I think I left them at the brownie stall. They were giving out free samples and I took my gloves off to try them. Here, hold these bags for me and I'll be right back.'

He handed her Ivy and the bags and took off at a run before she could even suggest that she would come with him. Suddenly a loose dog came charging through the market, barged into her and some of the bags she was holding fell to the floor. Luckily only soft things, like the scarf he'd bought for Carrie and the soft snowman toy she'd bought for Ocean. She folded the scarf neatly and popped it back into the bag and she spotted Shay's gloves at the bottom. He'd obviously taken them off at the brownie stall and popped them in one of his bags, out of the way and then forgot. She doubled back to try and find him and tell him. But he wasn't at the brownie stall. She wandered on a bit further, hoping he wasn't visiting every stall he'd visited in search for his lost gloves.

Then she spotted him at the antique jewellery stall, and he was clearly buying something. Something that was in a small, square box, which he slipped into his coat pocket. He'd bought an engagement ring. Her heart thundered in her chest. She wasn't ready for a proposal. It was too soon, but how could she say no to him when she'd wanted this all her life?

She quickly turned back before he saw her and made her way back to where he'd left her. What was she going to do?

She saw him walking towards her with a big smile on his face and she quickly plastered a smile on her own so he wouldn't suspect that she knew.

'I couldn't find them,' Shay said. 'I think I might have left them in one of my bags.' He took the bags from her and looked in a few and then found them. 'Oh look, here they are.'

Orla forced out a laugh. 'Oh, you daft sod, you should have checked them before you ran off.'

'I didn't remember putting them in there. Oh well, at least they're not lost. Shall we do this side of the market now?'

She nodded and he took her hand again but as they walked towards the other half of the market, her heart was racing. She had to say no, she wasn't ready for this. But she didn't want to hurt him and she didn't want the relationship to come to an end. She just wasn't ready for that step.

She saw Fern and Fletcher up ahead, with Bones, and Ocean fast asleep on Fletcher's shoulder. She let go of Shay's hand and ran over to give Fern a hug.

'Help me,' Orla whispered in Fern's ear.

Fern pulled back to look at her and nodded.

'We're going to get some hot chocolates, you boys stay here, we'll be back in a minute,' Fern said, linking arms with Orla and walking away before they got a chance to say anything.

'What's going on?' Fern said in concern once they were far enough away not to be heard.

'I think Shay is going to propose.' She explained how she'd seen him looking at engagement rings and how she'd caught him buying something from the jewellery stall. Something that came in a small square box.

'I have to say that I was where you are a few years ago, Ettie thought she saw Fletcher buy an engagement ring, I got swept away with the excitement and Mum persuaded me to buy a wedding dress and there was no proposal. And Shay took sixteen years to tell you he loves you; I don't think he's the kind to suddenly propose after a few days so before you get excited—'

'I'm not excited, I'm freaking out. It's too soon, isn't it? I know you got engaged after a month and Ettie got engaged in less than a week and you two are both blissfully happy, and I guess if you know this is your person there isn't any point in hanging around, but it feels too soon.'

'Do you doubt that Shay is the right one for you?'

Orla sighed. 'No, I love him with everything I have. He is the person that I want to raise a family with, grow old and grey with. I want what you, Ettie and Roo have, and he is the only person I've ever wanted that with.'

'Then what's the problem. *If* he proposes. You love him, he loves you. There is no right time when it comes to love, it's just whatever feels right for you.'

'I'm scared. I know there's no guarantees when it

comes to love, but right now this feels safe. I haven't even told him I love him yet because I'm trying to protect myself. If it comes to an end, if Shay decides he doesn't love me after all, it feels like we could easily just fall back into being friends again – we tried, nothing ventured, nothing gained, it didn't work, no big deal.' Orla swallowed a lump of emotion at that thought. It was definitely going to be a big deal; she was deluding herself if she thought she wouldn't get hurt. 'But if we get married and he walks away after a few months it would be so much worse. We talked about it. Marriage is a big commitment for me. It's not something I would enter into lightly after seeing how easily and how horribly it went wrong for my own parents. If I marry him, I have to be one hundred per cent convinced that it's forever and right now I don't trust that it is.'

They joined the queue for the hot chocolates and Fern was silent for a while, but eventually she spoke.

'If I'm being honest, I think the thing that is going to cause your relationship to fail is that you are holding back. You're trying to protect yourself by not telling Shay you love him but eventually that will start to cause doubt in his mind that this is a one-sided relationship and he will end it. He's already grown up in a relationship where there was no love, where his love for his mum was never reciprocated. He was a kid back then and he never knew he deserved better. But now he's confident enough to walk away.'

Orla gave a little gasp at that. She would never want to do anything to hurt Shay, she'd hate for him to walk away from this thinking he wasn't loved, that he wasn't enough because that wasn't the case at all. And she never realised she was self-sabotaging this relationship before it had properly begun.

'If you don't trust him because of something that happened twelve years ago before he got all that counselling, before he grew up to be the man he is today, then you probably need to talk to him about that and see if you can move forward from it. Because if you can't then it might be best to call a halt on this relationship now. Holding back is not fair on him and it's not fair on you. Neither of you are going to get what you want out of this unless you can go all in. If you're always waiting for it to end, then one day it will. You have to give one hundred per cent of yourself to him, and I don't mean marriage, but embrace the relationship without any doubts or fears. Give your heart to him fully.'

Fern was right, she was still living with her past demons and she needed to let them go. Could she do that, could she finally let go of the past for good and move on with the future she had always dreamed of?

'Everything has moved so fast for you two, well, sixteen years after it first started, but the last few days have been a blur. You've gone from being friends who loved each other from afar, to nearly dying in an accident, to Shay telling you he loved you, to making love and now you're practically living with him. I can understand you feel like you have whiplash from how fast things are moving. If I were you, I think you need to go back home, have some space away from him just for a day or so, get your head around whether this is something you really want. I think you're still in love with the boy that broke your heart, which is why you can't move on from that. You need to decide whether you're in love with the man he is now and whether you can trust him.'

Maybe this was part of her fear – it had all happened so fast. She'd never had a relationship like this that had gone from nought to ninety in less than a few seconds. Every man she'd dated in the past had started off slow, they'd been on dates where they'd got to know each other, then there had been the flirting, slowly becoming comfortable with each other. Even sex had always been OK to start with until they'd got to know each other's bodies, their likes and dislikes. It had never been mind-blowing from the first time like it had been with Shay. She'd never had a relationship with a man where they'd talked about marriage and children, she'd never reached the stage in a relationship where she wanted to live with a man or stayed longer than a night or a weekend at most. She'd had all that with Shay and it hadn't even been a week.

Everything had changed in a blink of an eye, and she was still trying to get her head around her new reality. Sometimes at night, she'd lie in his arms and wonder if this was all a blissful dream that she was going to wake up from at any minute. She couldn't quite believe that she got to kiss him, touch him, make love to him after all these years. And everything had been so deliciously perfect. The ease she had with him, they could chat for hours or not chat at all, and both were easy and comfortable because they knew each other so well. The sweet touches of affection had been wonderful; the cuddles, the kissing, the holding hands, the making love. Oh, the making love had been exquisite every single time, the way he worshipped and adored her body had been magnificent. Even staying in his house had felt so right, like she belonged there with him. She could picture herself there with him very happily for the rest of her life, even raising a family there.

And that was really the crux of the problem. Because everything had been so perfect she was scared of losing it all and the more time she spent with him and the more she fell in love with him, she held herself back even more.

But Fern was right, it wasn't fair on Shay. How must he be feeling every time he told her he loved her and she didn't say it back? How long would it be before he started pulling away too, to protect himself.

Maybe Fern was right; maybe a few days away from him would be good to give her a little perspective.

She nodded. 'I do love him, but a few days away would be good to get some clarity. The more I'm with him the more I'm scared of losing him. It's self-destructive and it's not fair. I need some time to figure out how to get past this before I ruin it completely.'

'I think that's a wise thing to do. But remember what I said about concussion causing unstable emotions. All of your worries about your relationship could be stemming from that. Maybe now isn't even the best time to start a relationship or make rational decisions, maybe you need to have a break for a few weeks until you start feeling more like you.'

She suddenly felt relieved about that. All of her worries and anxiety about the relationship ending could be coming from her concussion or at least it was heightening those concerns into something more. She had felt emotional and even tearful. Fern was right, this was just normal post-concussion symptoms. But she didn't need a few weeks to work out whether she loved Shay, she had loved him as long as she'd known him. She was going to fight for him, and for them, she just needed a few days away from him to work out how to do that.

Now she just had to tell him she was going home, and she wasn't looking forward to that.

Shay lay in his bed with Orla sprawled out on top of him as he tried to catch his breath. Orla's heart was still racing after he'd made love to her and he couldn't be any happier right now. He stroked his fingers up and down her spine and she moaned softly. He hadn't said he loved her today. He felt the awkwardness of it every time he did and she didn't say it back. He didn't want to pressure her into saying it if she didn't feel that way, but his heart was so full of her, it felt like it would burst. He wanted to shout it from the rooftops.

And he knew she had strong feelings for him; he could tell that by the way she looked at him, especially when they were making love. He just hoped that eventually she would feel the same way as him.

She moved onto her side but still cuddled against him.

She ran her hand over his chest and placed a kiss against his heart.

'I need to go home tomorrow,' Orla said.

He frowned in confusion. 'To get some more clothes?'

'No.'

He felt goosebumps on his skin. 'You don't have to, you can stay as long as you want. I love having you here. Hell, you can move in permanently if you want.'

'I do have to go. I... need some space to think.'

That didn't sound good.

He looked at her, stroking a hair from her face. 'Is something wrong?'

'No. Well yes but not with you, you haven't done anything wrong. You're the perfect boyfriend and I...' she paused. 'Will you trust me when I say I'm doing this for us?'

'I trust you completely.'

Tears filled her eyes.

'Hey, what's wrong?'

'Nothing,' she wiped the tears away. 'I'm fine. Fern thinks my emotions are all over the place because of post-concussion stress. She said she had that after she knocked herself out on her bike as a kid.'

He stroked her face. 'She did, she was crying all the time for no reason. It passed after a few weeks. Do you feel sad?'

'I feel worried and anxious.'

'About what?'

'It doesn't matter.'

'Of course it does.'

She reached up and kissed him, cupping his face and stroking it with her thumb. She pulled back slightly. 'I'm going to fix this, I promise. Just give me a few days.'

'Tomorrow is Christmas Eve, are we not going to spend Christmas together?'

'I'll see you at your mum's for lunch on Christmas Day.'

This wasn't what he'd planned at all for their first Christmas together but if she needed space then he had to respect that. But for the first time since they got together a seed of doubt grew in his heart. What if this was the beginning of the end?

CHAPTER TWENTY-SEVEN

Orla walked back into her flat the next morning. Theo had very kindly brought her home as Shay still didn't have a car. She'd said goodbye to Shay at his house, partly so Theo wouldn't have to take Shay back home again and partly because she knew Shay would want to come inside and she wanted that space to think. Theo hadn't said a lot to her – he probably didn't understand why she was going home the day before Christmas rather than spending it with the man she loved – and now she was here alone, she was beginning to question that herself.

She loved Shay, she knew that, she'd always loved him. That love had grown so much over the years that he was part of every breath, every thought. Her love for him was now almost part of her identity as much as her red hair and green eyes, her love of vintage jewellery or her favourite truffle pizza and her love of black and white films. It was something she always carried with her.

Impossibly, her love for him had deepened over the last few days. Why did she think not telling him how she felt would protect her if it came to an end. It would hurt either way. The only thing not telling him had achieved was hurting Shay, making him believe she didn't feel the same. All because she was so scared of it coming to an end.

Why was she so fearful about that, why couldn't she just enjoy what she had? She didn't walk down the street fearful of getting hit by a bus, she didn't get on a plane and panic that it would suddenly fall out of the sky. By rights, she should be scared about getting back in a car again after the accident, which had been very traumatic, but she hadn't given that another thought.

She knew that some of her anxiety was attributed to the injuries sustained in the accident. She'd even looked it up after speaking to Fern the night before and feeling sad or tearful or worried was very common after concussion. But those fears were there already, she knew that. The accident had just made them seem so much worse.

She sat down on the sofa and glanced across at the photo of her parents together on a family holiday to Greece when she was nine or ten. They looked so happy. She didn't know why she kept that photo – they had hated each other for probably eighteen years or more. They didn't even speak to each other anymore. But it reminded her of happier times. Her parents had looked so in love in this picture, as if nothing could ever break them. She'd seen how blissfully in love they were, always touching each other, holding hands, kissing, laughing together.

They were the three musketeers, they went every-where, did everything together and she loved those times.

Until her dad had cheated on her mum.

And in a moment of clarity, she suddenly knew that was where her fear came from. She'd been there when her mum had found out, she'd seen the moment her mum's heart had broken forever, she'd seen the agony and the complete and utter devastation.

Except it hadn't just been her mum that had been hurt by her dad's betrayal. Overnight, she'd lost the secure happy little family unit she'd grown up with. There had been no more family days out or holidays, no more camping and cuddling with each other under the stars, there had been no more family movie nights where they'd cuddle up on the sofa under the blankets, even the meal times where they'd sit around the table and talk about their day had gone. For several years she'd been alone while her parents fought like cat and dog. Even moving to Apple Hill Bay hadn't changed their attitude towards each other. It was weird to feel so utterly alone when she was living in the house with two other people, but she had. That was until she'd met Shay. He'd been her harbour in the storm.

She'd told Shay that what happened with her parents hadn't put her off marriage and that was true, she wanted to get married one day but she never wanted to go through the kind of pain of realising the person you love with everything you had, didn't love you back.

Except she already had when Shay had told her he didn't love her. And it didn't happen because Shay had been unfaithful. Every fibre of her being knew that Shay would never be unfaithful to her. She was sure thousands of men and women had said the same thing and had then been proved wrong, but she knew with every part of her heart and soul that he wouldn't do that to her. It had happened because he didn't think he was good enough for her, because he thought being with him would ruin her life. And as upsetting, frustrating and misguided those thoughts were, she did love him a little for it. He'd been trying to protect her after all, just like he'd always done.

In fact, everything he'd done had been because he loved and cared for her. Coming down to the beach with her almost every night because he didn't want her to be alone, standing up to her parents when she'd got hurt in one of their many fights, telling her he'd take her home from that party rather than spend the night with his girl-friend, being so fiercely protective of her when he found her with Kirk, that first weekend they spent together because he'd wanted her first time to be with someone who cared and respected her, telling her he didn't love her because he didn't think he was good enough, getting counselling because he wanted to be a better man for her. She even wondered if he'd bought Starlight Cottage for her because she'd always said she wanted to live it in one day. Everything had been for her.

Tears filled her eyes. He loved her so much and always had. It didn't make sense for her to worry about it ending when he'd given her no reason to think it ever would or any reason to doubt him at all. She had to let go of the hurt he'd caused her when he said he didn't love her, because his pain at the time had been worse and she understood why he'd done it.

She had been worried about losing him as a friend if it came to an end, but knowing how painful it had been to lose him the first time would ensure that wouldn't happen again, but now she realised she had been holding back, not just because of what happened when she told him she loved him but because of what happened with her parents. That had scarred her in ways she hadn't realised. Relief flooded through her and it was like a huge weight had been lifted from her shoulders. Her mum's story was not her own. And Shay was nothing like her dad. Realising where her pain had come from, she suddenly felt like she could move on from it once and for all.

She loved Shay and she wanted a future with him more than anything. If he was planning on proposing to her, it was a demonstration of his commitment to their future and she wanted to show him the same, that she was all in with him. She wanted to show him, not just tell him, he was loved and that he was hers forever.

She stood up and looked around. She had a plan.

Shay watched impatiently as the taxi pulled up outside Orla's flat. Coming here after he'd said he respected her need for space was either going to be a massive mistake or the most important thing he'd ever done.

The taxi stopped and Shay quickly paid and got out. Orla's flat was on the ground floor of a small block of six flats and he strode along the short walkway and knocked on the door. She opened it a few seconds later and her whole face lit up at seeing him. She threw her arms round his neck and hugged him tight. He wrapped his arms around her but when she showed no signs of letting go, he shuffled her back inside and closed the door behind him. She still didn't let go of him and he knew he'd made the right decision in coming here. He held her tighter, stroking her hair.

'What are you doing here?' she said, eventually. She pulled back slightly to look at him and he could see she was crying although she had the biggest smile on her face.

He stroked the tears away. 'I didn't want you to be alone. If you're feeling sad or anxious, then you need to be with someone and that doesn't necessarily need to be me – I know it's Christmas Eve, but Fern, Roo or Ettie would gladly have you round and keep you company. Even Carrie would welcome you with open arms if you needed a space, but you shouldn't be alone.'

Her smile grew and she hugged him again. 'I don't know how I got so lucky to find you, but you're the most wonderful man I've ever met.'

He held her tight. 'I will always be here for you.'

'I know.'

He pulled back. 'And if you have concerns about our relationship then we need to talk about them together. The only way this will work is if we're honest with each other.'

'I know, I didn't want to hurt you, and I thought I needed some time alone to think, but I should have told you what I was feeling. However, half an hour alone this morning and everything became so clear. And I have lots that I want to say to you. In fact, I had a big speech planned, although now you're here I'm going to have to rework it. Come on, we should go.'

She pulled away and grabbed her bag and coat and ushered him outside, but before she closed the door behind her, he noticed how empty her place was. The furniture was still there but all the pictures and knick-knacks that made the place hers were gone. He frowned in confusion and then quickly followed her out to her car.

He gestured back to her flat, as he was about to ask her about her things, but she was already getting in the car as if she had somewhere she was desperate to be.

'Come on, I'll give you a lift, it's on the way,' she laughed, but he had no idea what she was laughing at.

He got in her car, and she started driving the short distance to his house. He had no idea what was going on here. He glanced into the back seat and the bottom dropped out of his world. Every inch of it was filled with all her stuff, suitcases crammed with her clothes, boxes with all her photos and bits.

'You're leaving.'

'I'm going home,' she said, with the biggest grin on her face.

'Apple Hill Bay is your home.'

She pulled a face. 'Not really. I love it here, but it's not home.'

Panic filled him, did she mean she was going back to Ireland? That hadn't been home for her since she was a child. Was she going to London? After everything she'd said at the start of their relationship where she said that no matter what she didn't want to lose him as a friend, her running away now didn't make any sense.

She drew to a stop outside his house, and he took her hand. 'Look, I'm not belittling what you're going through, I totally get you're feeling emotional and maybe confused after the accident, but do you think you're in the right frame of mind to make big life changing decisions?'

'You're right, my emotions are all over the place and I have these periods, especially when I'm worried or excited that I can't seem to get my thoughts in the right order. But this, I have never been so certain of anything in my life. Come on, we should talk.'

She got out of the car and walked towards his house. He quickly followed and let her in. Ivy greeted him as if he'd been gone days not just fifteen minutes, then charged off upstairs, no doubt to cause more puppy mayhem.

He threw a few logs in the fire and added some kindling while he played for time. He had no idea what was going on and what he could say but he felt like he was on the verge of losing everything. He lit the fire and stared at the flames for a few moments.

He turned back to face her and she was beaming ear to ear. She frowned when she saw his expression. 'I thought you'd be happy.'

'Happy?'

'Oh my god,' she put her hands to her face. 'I forgot the most important part. I had this big speech planned, I've been rehearsing it for the last few hours as I packed. Then you threw me off by arriving at my house when I wasn't expecting you and then you made me cry by hugging me and being there for me as you always are and everything I wanted to say went out the window.' She reached up and stroked his face. 'I love you, I've always loved you, I love you so much it fills my heart to the top.'

'Then why are you leaving?'

She frowned in confusion. 'I'm not leaving.'

'You said you were going home.'

'I am home.'

Cautious hope filled his heart. 'You mean Starlight Cottage.'

'No, I mean with you. You are my home, Shay Lucas. It's always been you.'

Tears filled his own eyes. 'Oh god, Orla I thought you were running away again.'

'Oh Shay, no, I love you. Christ, the most important moment of my life and I screwed it up, rambling like a fool. I promise it's the concussion, it will pass.'

He wrapped his arms around her. 'And I'll be here to hold you until it does. I love you too. You are my entire world.'

He kissed her and felt the relief rush through him. She was home. He lifted her off her feet and lay her down in front of the fire. Pulling off her top, he kissed her neck.

'Wait, I have more things I wanted to say,' Orla said, pulling his jumper over his head, sliding her fingers up his bare back under his t-shirt.

'Later,' he said and kissed her again and this time she didn't protest.

✳

The fire was crackling happily next to them, the lights were twinkling on the Christmas tree and Orla couldn't have felt more happy wrapped in Shay's arms as they lay on the rug where he'd made love to her. Twice.

'Do you want to talk to me about what you were worried about?' Shay said, stroking his fingers up and down her spine.

'Yes, but please bear in mind that every worry has been heightened by the concussion.'

'I know, I imagine it's been a stressful few days.'

'It has,' she laughed. 'I felt myself panicking the other day when we were making the cookies with Ocean whether I'd got the ingredients right and I've been making cookies like that all my life, so everything has felt ten times worse. But from the very beginning of our relationship, I was scared it would come to an end. I felt like if I held back from telling you I loved you I couldn't get hurt, which was ridiculous because being with you brings me so much joy, it was going to hurt if it ended whether I'd told you or not. Yesterday at the market, when you went off to get your gloves, I dropped the bags and saw your gloves inside, so I went off to find you and saw you buying something from the jewellery stand.'

'Ah.'

'I freaked out because I thought you were buying an engagement ring, especially after I'd seen you looking at them a short while before while I was looking at the necklaces. I was scared you were going to propose because I felt if it came to an end now or in the next few weeks or months, it would hurt but I'd be OK, but if we got married and it came to an end it would be ten times worse.'

He smiled, wistfully. 'I want nothing more than to marry you and raise a family with you one day but even I wouldn't propose after a few days. I was looking at engagement rings, but purely because I was wondering what style I would buy for you, *when* I did eventually propose. But were you scared because I'd broken your heart before, is that the crux of all this?'

'I think that was a tiny part of it, not trusting that your feelings were real or at least big enough to last a lifetime.'

'Trust me, my love for you is big enough to last ten lifetimes.'

She grinned. 'I know because I feel the same. But actually, when I analysed why I felt so scared of it this morning, it came back to what happened to my parents and how devastated my mum was when she found out my dad had betrayed her. And how I felt when our lovely, happy little family unit was lost, all those family days out, the family holidays, the movie nights, gone in the blink of an eye, and that feeling of being utterly alone. What I have with you is everything, it's everything I've always wanted and dreamed about and now suddenly I have it and I was scared of the heartbreak I would feel if I lost it.'

He frowned, stroking her face. 'I would never betray you like that. I love you too much, I could never do anything like that to hurt you.'

'I know. As I said, I *was* scared, but I'm not anymore. Our story is different to theirs, we've been in love for sixteen years. I remembered everything you've done for me over the years that shows how much you love me, the little things, the big things, it was written in everything you did. I have no reason to doubt you or any reason to fear it will come to an end.'

'I know I shouldn't guarantee you a lifetime of being together. People change, circumstances change, but in my heart, I know this is forever for us, we have something rare and special,' Shay said.

'I feel that too.'

He kissed her and she couldn't help smiling against his lips.

'Would you like to see what I did buy you at the market?'

She nodded. He got up and she had the pleasure of watching him walk spectacularly naked across the room. He grabbed the box from his coat pocket and brought it back to her. She sat up and he sat down in front of her, offering out the box. She opened it and smiled when she saw the marcasite owl necklace she had been pining for.

'Oh Shay, I love it, thank you.'

'Happy Christmas baby.'

She leaned forward and kissed him hard. He wrapped his arms around her and fell back against the floor taking her with him.

'So you really do love it, you're not disappointed it isn't an engagement ring?'

'I love it,' she slid her hand down across his stomach and then moved it lower. 'And I'm going to show you how much.'

CHAPTER TWENTY-EIGHT

Orla was sitting on Shay's lap the next day at Carrie's house, watching Ocean chasing Bones, Clarke and Ivy. Her heart fell so full that she thought it might burst. Although that wasn't the only thing that felt like it could burst. They had eaten so much turkey and trimmings, plus the pre-lunch snacks, the desserts and copious amounts of chocolate. She didn't think she would need to eat for a week or more, she was so stuffed.

They'd opened presents, played games and watched several Christmas movies and she felt so lucky to be part of this wonderful family. Although right now, she'd quite like to go home with Shay, sleep for a few hours and then spend the rest of Christmas Day making love to the man she loved with all her heart. She wondered when would be an appropriate time to make their excuses and leave.

She'd had a long chat with Fern and told her everything she'd shared with Shay, and Fern couldn't have been happier for her that she'd finally put away her demons from the past. Carrie had spent every available opportunity talking about marriage and children and subtly and not-so-subtly asking when they were going to tie the knot.

'Do you want to go?' Shay whispered in her ear.

She looked at him and saw the dark look in his eyes that left her with no doubt why he wanted to go home. She nodded keenly.

'Mum, I think we're going to take off,' Shay said. 'We're both still a bit tired after the accident.'

'Yes of course, you must get some rest,' Carrie said.

Orla smirked, knowing rest was the very last thing on Shay's mind.

'But before you do, let's have a toast.'

Carrie spent a few minutes pouring and serving several glasses of sparkling wine and orange juice for those that were either driving or pregnant or too young to drink. Carrie finally held up her own glass. 'To happy ever afters.'

Carrie held her glass up to Antonio, then Fern, Fletcher and Ocean, then Theo and Roo and finally to Shay and Orla.

And everyone echoed her toast together, 'To happy ever afters.'

If you enjoyed *Christmas Wishes at Cranberry Cove*, you'll

love my next gorgeously romantic story, *The House on Waterfall Hill*. It's a brand new series set in Lovegrove Bay and it's out in Spring 2025

ALSO BY HOLLY MARTIN

Lovegrove Bay Series

The House on Waterfall Hill

Midnight Village Series

The Midnight Village

Meet Me at Midnight

Apple Hill Bay Series

Sunshine and Secrets at Blackberry Beach

The Cottage on Strawberry Sands

Christmas Wishes at Cranberry Cove

Wishing Wood Series

The Blossom Tree Cottage

The Wisteria Tree Cottage

The Christmas Tree Cottage

Jewel Island Series

Sunrise over Sapphire Bay

Autumn Skies over Ruby Falls

Ice Creams at Emerald Cove

Sunlight over Crystal Sands

Mistletoe at Moonstone Lake

The Happiness Series

The Little Village of Happiness

The Gift of Happiness

The Summer of Chasing Dreams

Sandcastle Bay Series

The Holiday Cottage by the Sea

The Cottage on Sunshine Beach

Coming Home to Maple Cottage

Hope Island Series

Spring at Blueberry Bay

Summer at Buttercup Beach

Christmas at Mistletoe Cove

Juniper Island Series

Christmas Under a Cranberry Sky

A Town Called Christmas

White Cliff Bay Series

Christmas at Lilac Cottage

Snowflakes on Silver Cove

Summer at Rose Island

Standalone Stories

The Secrets of Clover Castle (Previously published as Fairytale Beginnings)

The Guestbook at Willow Cottage

One Hundred Proposals

One Hundred Christmas Proposals

Tied Up With Love

A Home on Bramble Hill (Previously published as Beneath the Moon and Stars

For Young Adults

The Sentinel Series

A LETTER FROM HOLLY

Thank you so much for reading *Christmas Wishes at Cranberry Cove,* I had so much fun writing this story, revisiting the wonderful Apple Hill Bay and finally telling Shay and Orla's beautiful story. I hope you enjoyed reading it as much as I enjoyed writing it.

One of the best parts of writing comes from seeing the reaction from readers. Did it make you smile or laugh, did it make you cry, hopefully happy tears? Did you fall in love with Shay and Orla and the residents of Apple Hill Bay as much as I did? I would absolutely love it if you could leave a short review on Amazon. Getting feedback from readers is amazing and it also helps to persuade other readers to pick up one of my books for the first time.

If you enjoyed *Christmas Wishes at Cranberry Cove,* you'll love my next gorgeously romantic story, *The House on Waterfall Hill.* It's a brand new series set in Lovegrove Bay but as with all my series, all the books can be read as a standalone story.

Thank you for reading.

Love Holly x

STAY IN TOUCH...

To keep up to date with the latest news on my releases, just go to the link below to sign up for my newsletter. You'll also get two FREE short stories, booky news and be able to take part in exclusive giveaways. Your email will never be shared with anyone else and you can unsubscribe at any time https://www.subscribepage.com/hollymartinsignup

Website: https://hollymartin-author.com/
Email: holly@hollymartin-author.com
Facebook: facebook.com/hollymartinauthor
Instagram: instagram.com/hollymartin_author
Twitter/X: x.com/HollyMAuthor

978-1-913616-60-1 Paperback
978-1-913616-61-8 Large Print paperback
978-1-913616-62-5 Hardback
978-1-913616-63-2 Audiobook

Cover design by Emma Rogers

Made in the USA
Las Vegas, NV
12 November 2024

11659431R00159